The Night Human Heir

The Hunter Trilogy

Book 2

B. Kristin McMichael

The Night Human Heir
Copyright © 2018 by B. Kristin McMichael
www.bkristinmcmichael.com
All rights reserved.

LEXIA
·PRESS·
Lexia Press, LLC
P.O. Box 982
Worthington, OH 43085
www.lexiapress.com

ISBN-10: 1-941745-70-9
ISBN-13: 978-1-941745-70-0

Cover design: Jessica Allain
Editors: Kathie Middlemiss of Kat's Eye Editing
Melissa of There For You Editing
Ashton M. Brammer

BOOKS BY B KRISTIN McMICHAEL

- To Stand Beside Her

Chalcedony Chronicles

- Carnelian
- Chrysoprase
- Aventurine
- Chrysocolla

The Night Human World series:

The Blue Eyes Trilogy (series 1)

- The Legend of the Blue Eyes
- Becoming a Legend
- Winning the Legend

The Day Human Trilogy (series 2)

- The Day Human Prince
- The Day Human King
- The Day Human Way

The Skinwalkers Witchling Trilogy (series 3)

- The Witchling's Apprentice
- The Wendigo Witchling
- The Witchling Seer

The Merworld Trilogy (series 4)

- Waves and Secrets
- Water and Blood
- Songs and Fins
- Scales and Legends

The Hunter Trilogy (series 5)

- The Night Human Hunter
- The Night Human Heir
- The Night Human Siblings

CONTENTS

CHAPTER 1

Jax looked up from the floor. He loved this brotherly bonding time with Beck, as the older night human beat the crap out of him. Well, he didn't exactly like getting beat up, but it was time spent getting to know his half-brother. Beck wiped his dark blond hair out of his bright blue eyes as a smile formed on his lips. Beck was enjoying himself, too, it seemed. Then again, Beck was the one that was barely breaking a sweat as he pounded on Jax.

"I told you this would be easier if you just agreed with our dear father and used his blood," Beck said as Jax was sprawled on the ground. Jax didn't plan on getting back up. He was done for the day.

Jax was used to having his butt kicked. He had spent his whole life training as a hunter, and his mother was intense about training. She'd order him to run ten miles after an exhausting kickboxing hour. More than a few dozen times she had broken bones on him during training. And she'd always leave his body sore from head to toe with bruises that he never thought would go away. She was the kind of person most people avoided due to that intensity. Beck was kicking his butt, but he was still playing easy.

"I'm not taking his blood again," Jax replied as he finally sat up. "And I'm done for today. Father asked to meet me in twenty minutes, and I need time to clean up."

Beck sat next to Jax on the ground.

"So what's it about his blood you don't like? Is it the extra strength? Everything too light when you pick it up? Maybe you don't like being quick. That's got to be it. You like your slow human body. What's so bad about using his blood?" Beck seemed genuinely confused. "It's like you don't want to be stronger, or you can't stand being a night human."

Both were legitimate, with the latter being a better reason than the first.

"The whole 'I can't turn it off' part. You seem to forget that since you rarely turn off your night human, but when I take his blood I can't turn it off. I'm stuck in night human form until it wears off." Jax hated the feeling of not being in control. Yes, the speed and strength were wonderful, but losing control wasn't. "Would you want to walk around all the time with a sign on your forehead that says 'Attack me because I'm special'?"

Beck shrugged. "Okay. You got me there. Though, really, I'm not sure why it's so horrible that you wouldn't use it. It wears off eventually."

"Before or after I have to feed?" Jax replied.

And that was the reality of the problem. Night humans had to feed on regular day humans since blood was essential to their survival. After spending his life hunting those who did just that, Jax wasn't comfortable with that aspect of his new life at all. If he stayed in night human form too long, he would eventually have to feed. He'd only had to do it once so far and was able to find some blood in the fridge in Wes' house, but he didn't want to rely on that. What if there wasn't blood there? Would he have to walk around with fangs and find someone to munch on? Yeah, Jax wasn't doing that. He might be part vampyre, but he was never going to feed like one. He was never going to completely be one. That was one promise to himself that he was going to keep. He didn't want to be a monster, and he was never going to allow himself to be one.

"Well, I'll let you go for now then," Beck said, as he rose and pulled Jax up with him. "But we'll meet back here in a couple hours to finish our lessons for today. We still need to go over pressure points again. Your mom might have shown you all she knows, but she isn't a night human. There are more places that can incapacitate night humans than the hunters teach."

Jax nodded. Their father had put Beck in charge of getting Jax up to speed on defending himself. Beck had learned everything directly from their shared father, and Jax was happy to have the younger version teaching him. Beck took his orders very seriously as he wanted to get back to his life also. For now, he was stuck babysitting Jax, making sure he didn't get himself killed. From the way Beck complained, that seemed to be a full-time job.

Jax showered and made it back to the main house just in time. After finding his father and deciding to stay with the vampyre, Jax had moved into his father's home, which consisted of a few-thousand-square-foot family home behind the spatial mansion that everyone else lived in. His father kept an office in the main mansion where he did all his business, but spent the rest of his time in the cozier house at the back of the property where Jax was more comfortable. Jax had grown up without a room to call his own as they moved every few months to track and kill night humans. Living in a house was always a dream, but now it was a reality.

Since Jax heard Wes talking to someone, he waited outside the door. Wes was a stickler for manners, and Jax caught on quickly that only he was given a second chance at everything. At least Jax was on time. Beck had been exuberant in letting Jax know when he had missed a few meals or was late for meeting his father's second-in-command. It was a first to be a couple minutes early. Jax sat down on the bench outside his father's office.

'Come on in,' Wes said mentally to Jax.

Jax still didn't know how his father did that since the only mental connection Jax had ever heard of was when you connected blood to blood, or you were mates, but it was on the long list of questions to ask. He had been raised on the day human side of things, and even though he knew at least a dozen ways to kill every night human he had studied, that didn't cover stuff the hunters felt they didn't need to know. Jax stood up and walked into the room.

"So, Jax, we've been talking about removing the seal the hunters put on you," Wes said nicely, motioning to the chair in front of his enormous desk for Jax to sit.

We? Jax looked around the room. No one was there. His father must have been talking on the phone.

"I spoke a bit more with my source, and they have a couple ideas as to where it might be. We still can't be sure, but we're getting closer. If your mother was still talking to me, it would be easier, but it seems that she plans to continue pretending I'm dead."

Jax just nodded and did his best to think of anything but the seal, or his mother for that matter. Pretending he was dead was better than the hate Jax had always felt she had for him. Jax was sure his father was snooping around his mind to see what he thought of both comments. Jax still didn't trust the vampyre or his own father. Night humans always had an agenda, and that included who their next meal would be.

When his father first mentioned that the hunters sealed the night human side inside of themselves, Jax had no idea what he was talking about. Everyone knew that a night human and a day human having a child would end up a night human, but it wasn't the case with hunters. Jax had stumbled upon the biggest hunter secret he was sure no one under the age of eighteen in the hunter clan knew about. Hunters all had children with night humans. It was the only way to pass on the hunter gene, yet somehow the offspring didn't end up being night humans. It was logical that there had to be a seal. Nothing else made sense otherwise. Night humans and day humans together always produced a night human. Jax was certain he and every other hunter out there were day humans. Jax had never seen a hunter turn into a night human like his brother Beck could do. Beck had claimed his mother was a hunter, but he had no idea why that part wasn't sealed inside of him.

Wes was anxious to remove the piece binding Jax to his day human side. Jax wasn't as anxious. He still hated the feeling of being a night human when the hunger

5

started. The other parts were fun and actually felt like being a superhuman, but the hunger wasn't. Jax would prefer to not have to deal with that. Wes tried to explain that it wasn't a problem, but Jax had spent his life hunting down night humans. He wasn't really eager to become one. It was going to take more than a few weeks to dull that side of him.

"And I've found the perfect motivation for you to want to break the seal." Wes smiled at Jax like he knew his son's hesitation no matter how much Jax covered his thoughts.

While Jax felt welcome in the vampyre world of his father, he still felt there was more that was hidden. Wes had a great tendency to avoid answering questions, and the most Jax had learned about the vampyre came from Beck, who wasn't a full-time vampyre. It turned out after not being the heir, Beck moved on to join a group of night humans who hunted rogue night humans. Now that sounded like fun to Jax, but it wasn't an option. He was his father's heir and had to stay around the man he still couldn't completely trust—his own father.

"Come out to the gardens, and I'll show you what I mean," Wes instructed as he stood up from his seat.

Jax followed him out to the back room and onto the patio. The elaborate gardens were large enough to keep the cottage Jax lived in hidden from the main house. It wasn't like it had to be hidden. The whole clan knew about it, but it was more like the gardens kept their house separate from the vampyre mansion.

"About three years ago we got a call from someone who needed night human blood. They had a sick child who couldn't be cured with just any night human blood. They needed really strong blood, and my name was mentioned. Being one of the last firsts, it is normal that people would look to me for answers."

Jax's father was more than rare, probably the rarest night human around. He was one of the first night humans ever made. Jax had tried to find out how old the man really was, but no one knew, or would tell him at least. He was pretty sure his father was older than dirt, but even Beck didn't know.

"Since I was in hiding," Wes continued as they walked through the orderly trimmed bushes, "I wasn't able to respond, but I took that human in once I found her since she was cast out of her family. She's been living here with us since. I've been using my blood to keep her alive, but that's all I can do for her. We've studied her with all our best scientists, and we're sure that I can't turn her nor can I heal her. My blood can only keep her one step away from death. But as it turns out, you can help. This poor girl has lived in pain for three years and has no family left. She wants to join the night human world, and if you can turn on your night human side, you'll be able to save her."

Jax had no idea what his father was talking about. There was no way Jax was going to create new night humans, and Wes had to sense that. Any talk of making a new branch in the clan to replace the traitor Hector, who had tried to kill Jax, was met with deaf ears. Jax wasn't accepting of the whole drinking blood part, let alone feeding someone his blood before killing them and then creating new night humans that would run around sucking blood, too. Wes led the way farther into the gardens.

"So here's the thing. My blood has kept her alive, but it seems to not be working as well as it used to. Where we were once able to only feed her once every six months, it turned to every month, and now every week. We don't know how much time she has left." It sounded dire.

"What about the night human leader? Why not her blood?" There was a council of night humans led by a very powerful night human. Her blood was considered magic and could heal almost anything. Jax had heard that it could regrow appendages.

"Arianna's blood was tried before they came to me. It turns out this girl needs the blood of a First. Arianna, while strong, isn't a First. She's actually the fourth generation of the dearg-dul. She has all the power of her family, but her blood is diluted. Mine isn't. Neither is yours. But it isn't really blood that she needs. She wants something only you can help her with, and that's if you can find out how to remove the seal the hunters put on you."

Jax was intrigued, but he kept a bored face on. He had no idea how removing his night human hunter seal would help anyone but himself and his father. Jax didn't want Wes to know he was trying to figure out his father's new scheme. Night humans loved their games. His father, while blood to Jax, still was a night human. Wes had yet to earn Jax's complete trust.

Wes led the way farther back into the garden and around the corner to a stone bench. Jax stopped in his tracks. A beautiful girl with long, blond curls sat with a blanket over her lap. Her thin arms moved delicately to smooth out the blanket. She appeared to be sick, but life still shone in her movements. Jax was stunned speechless. This was the girl Wes wanted him to help.

She looked up at him, and her lashes seemed to flutter as her smile grew.

Jax already knew who she was. He had no idea how or why she was there, but Jax swore to himself two years ago that if he ever saw her again, he would do anything to help her. Maybe his father knew this or maybe it was just a coincidence. He watched her in fascination. Jax was stuck. She was his childhood crush and fellow former hunter, Simone.

Jax stared at Simone. His heart had been broken when her family said she was dead three years ago, but when his sister told him in confidence that Simone was still alive, he had searched all over for her. There was a funeral and everything, but Jade explained it had been an empty casket. Simone had just disappeared. What better way to stay hidden than to live with an extinct night human clan? She had been perfectly hidden where no one would even think to look.

"I'll leave you two to get caught up," Wes commented as he faded back into the garden, the way they came only moments before. He had played his trump card, and Jax was out of options.

Standing in the quiet evening air, Jax could do nothing but stare. It was like a dream come true to see her again.

He had thought many times as to what he'd say or do if he saw her again, but nothing seemed to fit this moment. The hunters had all moved on, but he hadn't. His sister, Jade, hadn't either. There weren't a lot of hunters, and even fewer children. When they found someone their age, they tended to be friends and stay friends. Jade had been close friends with Simone, and Jax had had a crush on her for close to forever.

"You going to stand there all night staring at me, or are you going to sit down and catch up?" Simone finally asked, snapping Jax back to reality as she scooted a bit on the bench to make room for him.

Watching her move over, he hesitated to sit down. She was obviously very sick, and he didn't want to possibly hurt her. Simone slid over a bit more to make space for him without any hesitation. Jax carefully sat down, making sure not to bump her in the process. This wasn't the Simone he remembered. She had been strong just like all the female hunters and full of life the last time he saw her. It looked like now she would break at the slightest touch.

"Hey, stranger," Simone teased Jax, leaning over to punch him in the shoulder. It was as light as a fly landing. She didn't just look weak; her hunter strength was gone, too.

Schooling his face into a fake smile, Jax was at a loss for what to say. He had spent so much time on the computer searching everywhere for her. He broke into hospitals around the country where she had been on cases to see if she had been lost. Her family was adamant that she was dead and marked her death in the hunter cemetery. Jax mourned the loss of their friend, but it was Jade who refused to accept that. She was the one who bribed the worker in the cemetery to admit that the grave was empty. Now she was really sitting there next to him, and Jax had no clue what to say first.

"So I guess my mother has been going around telling everyone that I'm dead," Simone started for him, sensing his loss for words. "Must be strange to see someone alive that you thought was buried years ago ..."

"Not that strange since Jade found out that you weren't in the grave. Hunters always bury their own in the cemetery protected from night humans, and I have a better guess as to why now." He had to imagine the hunter cemeteries had some sort of protection on them to keep the hunters from becoming night humans like the vampyre who were raised from the dead. "If you weren't there, then you had to be alive. It didn't make sense to Jade and me, so we searched and searched, but we couldn't find a trace of you."

Simone beamed at Jax, and it made his heart melt. He would do anything to get a smile from her before, and getting one now so easily was the best reward. Simone was beautiful with a perfectly symmetrical face, pale porcelain skin, and beautiful sky blue eyes, but her smile just made it even more so.

"I knew you guys wouldn't let me disappear. I didn't want to either. I wanted to call you on more than one occasion to tell you where I was. Too bad I found a group that was already non-existent to join. The vampyre know how to hide. Otherwise, you would have been able to find me."

Jax nodded. The hunters thought the vampyre and Wes were extinct. He had no doubt he would have never found her if his father hadn't just handed her to him. Jax looked at Simone, but she averted her gaze as he met her eyes. Jax studied at her frail body and tried not to let his sadness show at seeing her like that. Hunters were strong and brave, not weak and breaking. He could have never imagined she or any hunter could appear to be so sick. Hunters didn't get sick, probably due to their night human side.

Simone picked at the blanket on her lap, and Jax took in the rest of her.

"Is what Wes says true?" Jax finally asked.

"Did he give you the whole 'she's dying' talk?"

Jax nodded. He was pretty sure just by looking at her that she was dying, but being rejected and left behind by the hunters was crazy. The hunters, while risk takers, were family. They protected their own, especially the girls. Hunters didn't have a lot of children and girls were the most valuable as they were the only ones with enough strength and stamina that could be full-time hunters. He had never heard of a single family walking away from their child.

"Well, he's right. I'm dying. I have been my whole life. He's been able to keep me alive a lot longer than I thought I'd be, but yes, I'm dying. I have cancer." Simone's big, blue eyes stared at Jax, waiting for his response.

"Impossible. Hunters don't get sick," Jax replied exactly as she had waited for.

"They don't get sick, but turns out I was born this

way. I've had cancer since I was born, but my parents didn't know about it. My hunter healing side had been fighting every day since I was born, and it finally lost a couple years ago. The cancer is winning, and I'm dying."

That was a lot to take in. Jax had been learning more about night humans since he had found his father but even more about hunters. It was getting more and more obvious that they kept all the children in the dark as they turned them into night human hunter monsters. Jax had to wonder what Jade would think of everything he had learned. Were they telling her more now, too? Or was she still left in the dark?

"Did your parents really abandon you?" Jax had a feeling what the answer was, but he needed to hear it from her.

"Yeah, pretty much. After they took me to see the night human Arianna and try her blood, they figured nothing would save me. They gave me a bunch of money and set me up in a hotel room to die. I assumed they planned to come back for my body, but they never did."

That was heartless, even by hunter standards.

"So how did Wes get involved?"

"I have no idea how he found me, but he did. He simply showed up at my hotel room and offered to take me with him to his home. I know how night humans are and not to trust them. I don't know why, but I trusted him. I could feel there were no bad intentions coming from him. He really just wanted to help me. I figured I was dying anyway, so it was the last chance. He explained how his blood was stronger than Arianna's blood, and I gave it a try. It was amazing. I felt normal again. The first time I took some of his blood I was ready to head back home. I made it as far as town, but when I noticed the crowd at the cemetery, I realized my parents had told everyone a lie. I wasn't sure how I was going to go home then; it seemed I wasn't exactly wanted back and we kind of worried that Wes' blood was going to change me into a night human. There's no way I'd be welcome home then. By taking blood to be saved, I became an outcast to the people I thought were family." Simone shrugged, but Jax heard the hurt. He had learned enough in the last couple weeks to know exactly how that felt. The hunters weren't what he ever thought they were.

"So you just stayed here? You never thought to contact Jade? She was devastated that you were gone, and more that you were missing." Jax wasn't mad at her. He completely understood the feeling of being betrayed by the hunters. He understood his place in the hunter world would never change, no matter how much stronger he became. Heck, he wouldn't be the father of his own kids if he stayed since he wasn't a night human. It was a messed-up world. The only good there was in the hunter world was his sister.

"If it wasn't your father that took me in, I would have called you. But I couldn't expose Wes. He was saving my life. It wouldn't be kind to repay him by disclosing he was still alive. He hid from the hunters on purpose. Did you know that your mother brings a hunting clan here to New Orleans once a year to hunt for him? She's the only one convinced he's still alive, and luckily no one else believes her or takes her seriously." Pausing, Simone studied Jax. He was surprised as he didn't know his mother had ever been in New Orleans, or even that she did it once a year. She acted like there was nothing to know about his father and as if she hadn't been searching for him the whole time.

"And she isn't the only one," Simone continued. "There are night humans who come in search of him every year also. Wes is a First, and many people want to get his blood. He has to stay hidden."

"Then he isn't doing a good job. We found him online easily," Jax stated, referring to his search with Jen only days before.

Simone smiled. "That's the best part. He stays hidden in plain sight. Everyone thinks he can't really be him and that he hired an imposter to pretend."

"And the vamps just sit around and let it go that way?" Jax had been around night humans enough to know they were all power hungry. Why would someone below him simply sit and wait when they could take him out with help and be the top of the group? One little rumor and they could be at the top of the clan.

Simone smiled. "They don't have a choice. When a First dies, they can choose to activate the bond with their sire. Every one of them would die alongside him if he chose that. The vampyre only live on after his death if he wants to let them. He has complete control of them."

Jax really needed lessons on what the first night humans were and what they could do. It seemed his hunter education skipped that much along with quite a bit else. They had been so focused on teaching him how to kill; he guessed they didn't have time for anything else. Still, it would have been nice.

Simone smiled at him, her blond lashes fluttering. He could see her shoulders sag a little bit as she peered over his shoulder. Someone was behind the bushes, waiting for them. Jax could tell it wasn't his father or brother, but it was a night human. His hand slid to the knife at his ankle. Reaching over, Simone stopped him by placing her delicate fingers on his arm.

"That's just Missy. She's the night human who takes care of me," Simone explained. A dark-haired vampyre stepped out of the shadows and nodded to Simone as if she had been mentally called. "My time out of bed is done, I guess."

Jax wanted to stop her, but he could see she was fading quickly. Whether Missy came on command or not, she was there to take care of Simone. Jax could see that Simone trusted the vampyre completely.

"Missy can smell when I'm getting too weak and need more blood. Your father ordered her to take care of me, and she knows her life is forfeit if she lets me die."

Jax nodded as he watched the vampyre cautiously approach Simone. That sounded like something his father would say. He didn't know the man too much but in the few weeks he had seen of him, his father made rules that came with dire consequences. Missy waited to be sure Jax wasn't going to stop her as she bent down to scoop Simone into her arms. He had to imagine she was as light as a doll. Simone smiled at Jax as she closed her eyes while taking a deep breath. She instantly went to sleep.

"How much time does she have left?" Jax asked quietly before the vampyre could walk away.

Missy looked up at Jax like she was surprised she was being addressed at all.

"We don't know, sir," she replied with a thick southern accent. "When she first came to us, we were feeding her a vial of blood once every few months. Then it was every month, then every week. We are now feeding her a bag of blood every other day. Mr. Cunningham has been storing his blood as he knew this would happen, but we don't know how much longer she will last or how long the blood will last. Only time will tell."

With no further questions, Jax nodded as the girl turned to carry Simone away. It broke his heart to see her so sick. All his memories were of fun times with her full of life. He never knew that she was sick, or that a hunter could die from disease. It was worse to know she was spending her last days alive without family. The hunters had just abandoned her. At least he was there now. She wouldn't be alone.

"Father expected this would be the kind of motivation you needed," Beck said as he materialized from the shadows.

Where Jax had noticed Missy approaching, he didn't sense Beck at all which was a trick he'd have to ask Beck to teach him someday when life wasn't as complicated as it was just now. Then again, that was one of many tricks he wanted to learn from Beck. While he was as strong as the hunters, there was something more about him that drew Jax to him. He didn't really know how old Beck was, but he was pretty sure he wasn't ancient like their father, yet he could come and go as easily as the old man.

Jax didn't reply to Beck's observation about what Jax already knew. Yes, Jax wasn't a fan of removing the seal and becoming a night human full time, and he was sure his father knew no matter how hard he tried to hide it. Maybe he could, or maybe it was just years of studying humans made it seem like Wes could read minds. It didn't really matter which it was. Jax wasn't sure removing the seal the hunters put on him was a good idea. It was ideal that Jax had no clue how it was done, because then he wasn't outright refusing the old vampyre. Now it seemed he was caught, since Simone clearly needed help.

"Would she get better if she was a night human?" Jax needed to hear they were certain.

"Yes. Night humans don't get cancer," Beck replied. "And that's the truth. Not the half-truth the hunters fed you all these years. If you haven't figured it out yet, they've been lying to you your whole life. If you want real answers, you are going to need to be free of them."

Beck made it sound so simple. It wasn't though, and Jax wasn't going to contradict his older brother. Beck seemed to be the only one Jax could trust in the vampyre world to tell him the whole truth. He had nothing to gain or lose if Jax did or didn't do what Wes wanted. Beck was truly the brother Jax always wanted.

"That's great and all, but you both don't seem to realize the truth of the matter. I'm a male. I was never privy to the hunter secrets. Your guess as to how the night human side is sealed in us is as good as mine."

And that was really it. Jax had no clue how they hid away the night human side to the point that none of the young hunters suspected their dads were night humans.

Beck nodded. "I figured that much. Time for a road trip, little brother. Let's go have some brotherly bonding time."

Beck's smile was full of mischief. Jax already knew what bonding time felt like with Beck. It included some new bruises every time Beck mentioned it.

Jax shook his head at his blond-haired grinning brother. "I'm going to regret this, won't I?"

Beck didn't answer as he turned to lead the way out of the garden. Jax caught a whiff of lavender as they left, and he glanced in the direction Simone had been carried. No matter his feelings on breaking the bond for himself, he needed to find an answer for her. Simone's life depended on it, and he wasn't about to let her die a second time.

CHAPTER 2

"**I really didn't** take you for the convertible type," Jax told Beck as his brother drove along Interstate 10. They were over twenty hours into their road trip and hadn't left the interstate yet. "Vampyre are supposed to melt in the sunlight."

"Which makes this the perfect disguise," Beck replied. Okay, that much was true.

"So why don't you?" Jax asked.

"Don't what?"

"Melt in the sunlight?"

"Because no one melts in sunlight," Beck answered like Jax was the idiot.

"Okay, not melt, but die. Why doesn't sunlight kill you? I've seen the other vampyre. They hide from the sun because it hurts them. Why can you be night human one moment and not the next?" Jax had met many of the vampyre since he had been staying with his father. None of them could do what Beck did.

"Because I'm a Second and was born this way," Beck replied like it was the perfect excuse. It really didn't explain anything for Jax. "Being our father's son, even if I'm not the heir, does have benefits."

"And the others?" Jax asked about the rest of the vampyre clan, which he had found was close to fourteen thousand members. Amazingly, fourteen thousand people that hid perfectly and pretended not to exist. He had no clue how, but they did it well enough to keep the hunters from finding them. What exactly were they considered if Jax was a Second?

"They are creations, just like most of the clans. Sometimes you need a direct line to create the lesser in your clan, and sometimes they can create each other. There are few born to the direct line as we are. So we get some special privileges."

Jax really needed a handbook on the vampyre. He had studied them only a little as he had of every clan that the hunters had cataloged, but because he had never hunted a vampyre before, he didn't know much in terms of details. He was finding the little he did know was completely insufficient and it wasn't like anyone was teaching him. Most of the vampyre hid from him, and the little he did glean was from watching the few that didn't notice him.

The sun was starting to set in the direction they drove. Jax had no clue where they were going or how long they would be gone. Beck didn't tell him to pack anything, but being a hunter meant that Jax was already ready to go at any time. He had enough clothing to get through a few days if they ever stopped. Their car ride was excruciatingly long, but at least as a vampyre, Beck needed very little sleep. And that was a good thing because he refused to let Jax drive. That had been the first of many arguments on the drive. And when Beck was done arguing, he simply used the card of being the older brother and in charge, and there was nothing Jax could do. An older brother sounded great in theory, but Jax was quickly finding out it wasn't as much fun in practice when he continually lost every argument because he was younger.

Jax wanted to ask when they would arrive at wherever they were going, but he kept his mouth shut. He had already asked once, and Beck's answer was that it wasn't of concern for Jax since he wasn't going to be driving at all. Jax found out pretty quickly that Beck would ignore him if he asked the same question that his brother felt had already been answered, so there was no point in asking again. Leaning back, Jax settled in to take another nap. It wasn't like he needed to be awake to man a map or anything. Beck didn't have GPS on.

Closing his eyes, Jax pretended to drift off to sleep, even though he wasn't remotely tired. He wanted to know more and hated to be kept in the dark. Using the silent time, Jax sifted through his thoughts on the past few weeks. It was crazy to know that his father was a night human, but crazier to know Jax wasn't one. That part was hard to understand. If you had a night human for a parent, you became one. End of story. There wasn't any way around it. Then why did the hunters stay normal day humans? Jax wanted to know the answer as much as his father did, but it wasn't because he wanted to be a night human. He just wanted to know how and why it was like that. If there was some great secret the hunters were keeping, then why couldn't his half-sister Jen be in on it? She didn't want to be a night human, and here Jax was, able to be normal while she couldn't. He had to believe that there would be hundreds, if not thousands, of people that would want in on the hunter secret. Maybe that's why it was a secret. They didn't want to share.

"Before you died, were you able to turn your night human side on and off?" Jax asked as he opened his eyes and sat back up. Sleep wasn't going to happen.

"No," Beck replied. "I was just a normal human."

"So maybe that's it. Maybe I need to die to be a night human," Jax suggested and instantly regretted such a thought. He didn't need Beck to get the impression he wanted to die. He might take him up on the offer.

"If that was the case, then every hunter out there would come back as a night human," Beck stated, destroying Jax's logic. Beck was right. Then again, it seemed Beck was always right.

Jax thought a bit more as Beck didn't offer any other solution. Jax had never heard of a hunter coming back to life as a night human. He was pretty sure that would be news he would have heard growing up, especially if it happened to each person that died. It wasn't uncommon for hunters to die before they reached fifty. His mother, at almost forty, was one of the older hunters. There had to be hundreds—if not more—buried beside his grandmother in the East Coast hunter cemetery.

"Maybe that's why they're buried at the hunter cemetery. That way they can't come back as a night human," Jax suggested. That made sense. Hunters were meticulous in making sure their dead were found and buried.

"That's not it either," Beck replied while still watching the road, easily dismissing Jax's new idea before he could make an argument. "While I do agree that every hunter I've ever met would be as horrified as you are at the prospect of being a night human, I'm certain the cemetery has nothing to do with it. In my line of work, I've seen many hunters die. It can take up to a week to get them home and into the cemetery. The vampyre change takes three days. I have a feeling the secret lies in how hunters live, not how they die."

"If that's the case, then why didn't you turn into a night human before you died? You weren't a hunter. Why were you normal?"

Beck leaned back and laughed. Jax didn't have the slightest clue what was funny about his question. Turning the wheel sharply, the car kicked up dust as Beck drove off the highway onto a dirt path.

"I was wondering how long it was going to take before you asked about my mother."

Jax hadn't asked that, but he wasn't about to interrupt. Beck wasn't one on oversharing, so Jax would let him talk as much as he wanted.

"If you couldn't tell by my chosen profession, hunting is in my blood." Beck didn't seem to mind the dust that was partially blocking his view. He paused a moment to let what he was saying sink in. "My mother was your aunt. I'm part hunter, just like you."

Jax stared at Beck as he pulled the car to park outside a rundown shack with a neon sign flashing "Open" over the door. Jax didn't care that they were now stopped; he was too busy staring at Beck like he had grown a second head. Jax hadn't studied Beck that closely before, but now he saw it. One little admission changed everything.

It wasn't just that Beck had Jax's mother's same honey blond hair and blue eyes. It was the shape of his eyes and the quirk of his smile. How could he have missed it? Beck was definitely more than just his half-brother. Beck was part hunter.

Jax couldn't help but sit and stare at Beck. It made so much more sense now. He knew a lot about the night human world and hunters. He knew because he was one. He was part hunter and part night human, just like Jax.

Rommy had never mentioned having a sister, but Jax and Jade knew better. All hunters had two children and only two children. They waited many years while growing up for their mother to tell them about her sibling, but she never did. In fact, no one in the hunter community mentioned Rommy having a brother or sister. Rommy had to have a sibling, so Jax and Jade tried to find their mother's lost sibling. They had expected to find her brother or sister buried in a hunter cemetery but had no such luck. Their mother hadn't just erased all talking about her sibling by anyone; there wasn't much left at all. Jax and Jade came to the conclusion that there wasn't a sibling. Their grandmother had been quite old by hunter standards when she had Rommy, so maybe she died before she could have a second child. At least that's what Jade and Jax came to believe.

"Okay. You can't just leave it at that. A hunter? My aunt? Why weren't you raised as a hunter? Why did we never hear about you? And for that matter, why don't you know how to get rid of the hunter bonds that keep me human if you did it yourself. I'm not needed to help Simone. You should be able to do that." Jax had to wonder now what their impromptu drive was all about.

Beck opened up his car door and walked away without saying a thing. Jax moved to follow, but Beck was already standing on the other side of his door. Stupid night human speed. Jax glared at Beck who had just dropped a bomb and then didn't answer any questions. The whole vampyre family seemed to take the secret thing way too far. Here they wanted him to become one of them, but at the same time, no one seemed willing to tell the whole truth.

Beck stared at Jax and Jax defiantly stared back. He wasn't backing down. He wanted answers.

"We'll talk about this later. Right now we need to get some answers." Beck acted like his word was final, and Jax was about to tell him it wasn't when Beck continued, "For Simone. Her time is almost up, and we need to figure this out."

Jax's words caught in his throat as the image of his dying friend came to mind. He wanted solutions, but they would have to wait. Jax knew as well as Beck did that her time was limited. He had seen it himself. She was dying.

"If you want to come in, you can't come as a hunter. They probably already sense you're here and most of them will attack first and ask questions later."

"They sense me?" Jax asked. That was the first he'd heard about that.

"It's more a general sensing thing, but as soon as they see you they will know what you are," Beck replied without a detailed explanation.

"So they don't have to touch me?" Jax had been used by the hunters for years because his touch could tell a night human from a day human.

"Most of the ones in there aren't the tactile sensing kind, but night humans, just like day humans, come in all kinds. There are some that can touch and sense a hunter the same way you can a night human, or others that can feel it by seeing or hearing. Just because they can't all sense you, enough will. So if you want to come in, you have to turn on your night human side." Beck stood blocking the door, giving Jax his "I'm-in-charge" look.

Normally Jax would go against anything he was told to do by a night human, but even without all the truth, Jax did trust Beck. He was pretty certain that his older brother had gotten him out of more than just the few skirmishes Jax had been in since coming to New Orleans. From the sounds of things he had overheard of Beck and their father, it seemed like Beck had gotten Jax out of more than a little trouble even before New Orleans; trouble Jax hadn't even known he was in.

Reaching down into his bag, Jax pulled out a thin plastic tube. It held the blood of his father and was the only thing that allowed his night human side free. Without hesitation, Jax tossed it into his mouth and crunched down, doing his best to ignore the metallic blood taste in his mouth. He would never get used to that part. The taste of blood coated his tongue, and he had to hold back a gag. He was never going to make a good night human when drinking blood repulsed him.

Beck stepped back from the door to allow Jax to leave

the car. Thanks, buddy, Jax wanted to add. Beck turned his back and led the way to the run-down shack beneath the neon blinking sign. There were letters missing from the name as if they were burnt out, leaving only a T, U, and Y. Jax wasn't sure if it was a bar or a diner or what, but he kept his mouth shut. As Jax stepped out of the car, Beck turned back around and tossed him something. Jax caught it. A baseball cap.

"To blend in, you need to be a night human, but that mark on your forehead is like a flashing beacon for someone to take you to use as a blood bag for the rest of your life."

Jax tried to not let his eyes bug at that comment. He had spent his life knowing that he could be targeted by night humans for his blood as night humans claimed hunter blood was extra good, but he never once thought that they would target him as a night human.

"Not all night humans are created equal. Your forehead says that much," Beck explained to Jax's unasked question. "Keep your head down. Don't speak in case someone can sense your power in your voice, and just follow my lead. I can keep you safe, but I really don't want to have to kill these guys. They are my sources of info for half my outside assignments."

Jax wasn't completely sure what Beck meant, but he was going to follow his brother's orders. At least until he figured out if Beck was telling the truth. Why would any night human attack another they thought was stronger? That made no sense. The stronger one would beat them. Night human life was based on power. He still wasn't sure about details, but he knew that much.

Pulling the cap on, Jax followed Beck through a front door that was missing a few boards along with the handle to open it. Beck just pushed, and the thing creaked on its hinges. Jax hated to go in blind, having no clue why they were where they were, but Beck was the silent type who wasn't going to share no matter how uncomfortable it made Jax.

Jax tried his best to keep his face down to keep the mark on his forehead hidden, but it was hard to not look around. It wasn't simply a bar filled with night humans. It was a bar filled with night humans openly in their night human forms. That wasn't something Jax saw too often.

There were places in the night human world where day humans and night humans coexisted, but for the most part, the creatures of the night hid from their food. If they had a possible day human form to hide in, that was what most of them would be. Not here. The bar was off the main road with no indication of what you would be stepping into if you didn't know about night humans. But then again, Jax wasn't sure what kind of person would stop at such a rundown place to begin with.

Beck led the way over to the bar, and Jax followed closely behind him. He had only glanced around the room, but he noticed most of the people looked casually at the door, passing over Beck and staring at Jax.

"Is JoJo in?" Beck called to the bartender, who was down the bar from the only open spot, which they were standing in.

Jax didn't have to look at the man next to him to know he was watching him; he could feel his eyes on him. Jax only half paid attention to Beck as he talked to the bartender, because it was the night human next to him that had him a bit more worried. He had been around the vampyre in his new night human form, but it was different now being around other night humans. It was like he felt much more than he ever knew was possible. And what he felt from the overweight man next to him had Jax on edge. It wasn't like he was afraid of going against a four-hundred-pound night human. Size wasn't really the problem. It was the intent that was. And this man was looking at Jax just like Beck had said. Jax was a prize.

Without missing a beat, Jax stepped back and felt the whoosh of air from someone swinging at him. The man had made his first move, and Jax was prepared thanks to his hunter training and hours spent with Beck. Before he had a chance to respond, the room silenced as Beck moved, almost impossible to detect, and took out three of the men in the room. Jax was pretty sure most of the people hadn't seen Beck moved. It was only from practice that he could even catch a glimpse of his half-brother. Jax wasn't sure his normal hunter eyes would have been able to track his brother when he ended up beside him on the side of the fat night human, who was now headless.

"For your information," Beck said loudly to the silent room, which was still not moving; some looked angry, but most appeared to be stunned, "this is my little brother, and anyone who wants him will have to go through me."

It was like the collective group of night humans were all waiting for Beck to do something else. Jax had a feeling it wasn't the first time they had seen him in action, but it was the first time he had seen his older brother's real power. Jax now realized that Beck was severely restraining himself when they were training together. He probably was decreasing his own strength by at least seventy-five percent or more. Jax had never watched their father in action, but if this was what a son that wasn't the heir could do, it left him wondering at his own possibilities.

"You sure know how to set the mood, sugar," a deep female voice said from behind Jax.

He spun around to find out who it was they were meeting and was surprised to discover the older hunter that had taken him on his only ever trip to New Orleans was standing there with an outstretched hand for Beck to shake. JoJo happened to be the hunter, JoAnne. Beck reached around Jax and clasped the woman's arm as they shared a greeting with their eyes.

"I suppose this is a private meeting," she added as the room around them burst back into motion. People still cast glances at Beck and Jax, but they didn't have the same hostile intent Jax had felt before.

"Always," Beck replied as he began to walk with Jo through the crowded bar to the wall lined with booths and tables. She grabbed a tray with drinks as she moved through the crowd, leading the way and balancing them effortlessly, like she did it a lot. Never in his life had Jax pictured her as a waitress. In fact, he couldn't picture a single hunter as a waitress.

Taking the last table in the corner farthest from the door, she dropped the drinks down. There were more than fifty night humans between their table and the exit; this was especially where Jax didn't want to be after finding that Beck wasn't kidding about the night humans wanting him, and he hadn't even taken his cap off. Jo sat down in one chair and Beck in the other, both facing the crowded room. It forced Jax to take the last chair where he would have his back to the night human monsters who filled the place … not the position he wanted at all.

"So is the kid really your brother or just a new trainee?" Jo asked as she reached to the salt shaker and turned it over, dusting the table. Leaning down, she exhaled over the crystals. Magic pulsated from the spilled salt.

"Yes, but not the one you think," Beck answered.

Jo questioned Beck with her eyes. Jax figured it was his turn to speak as he reached up and turned his hat around. It would still pretty much cover the mark on his forehead, but it would give her access to see his face. Jax stared at Jo as he waited to see what she would say.

Jo seemed to be momentarily shocked.

"I think you got that one wrong, Beck. He's your cousin, not your brother." Obviously, the hunters knew more than they ever told Jax or Jade. Jo had to know about Beck's mother, Jax's aunt.

"No. Turns out he's my cousin and my brother. When my mother left the hunters, they decided not to waste a great offer such as the one from Wes." Beck shrugged like that was all he knew on the subject; or rather, it was all he was going to share.

Jo burst out laughing.

"Of course. Rommy's defecting son would be your

brother. Now it all makes perfect sense." Jo slapped her knee as she laughed more. "You know, we were all wondering who their father was. She never would tell us. Some of the girls were jealous when Jade came into her own before her fourteenth birthday and tried to get it out of her. Now I understand why."

"Defecting?" Jax asked, ignoring the rest about his mother keeping his father not only a secret from Jax and Jade, but everyone.

"You can't think you're the first hunter child to run off seeking your father? And you can't think they would consider you still family now that you sided with night humans?"

Jax hadn't questioned whether others had left before. He'd just assumed families with one child had already lost their other daughter. Sons were rare in the hunter world, but it might have been more that sons who stuck around were rare. However, it did make sense. Especially since sons weren't needed in the hunter world. And the bit about not going back was already assumed. Hunters despised night humans. He knew he was never going back the moment he met his father and found out the truth, but to hear he wouldn't be welcomed was a bit of a shock. Regardless, he did his best to hide it.

"What are you two doing way out here?" Jo asked casually as her gaze flitted around the bar.

No matter how old she was, she was still a hunter, and her instincts had to be blaring with all the night humans around. Jax wondered what she was doing in a night human bar in the middle of nowhere, but again it was a question he knew Beck would never answer.

Jax turned to Beck, but it seemed his brother was shut off, as normal.

"We're attempting to find out how someone can get rid of whatever the hunters place on us to keep us human," Jax replied. "How to access our night human side."

Jo raised an eyebrow. "So not only defecting from the hunters, but you want to actually join the other side completely. Just playing around as one isn't enough for you? Now that's a new one. Most hunters can't stomach to be around their fathers for too long, let alone join them."

Jax shrugged. He was still getting used to things, but it wasn't as bad as what his mother had raised him to believe. Yes, the night humans were different, but it wasn't like they were all pure evil. But then again, Jax could always sense not just if someone was a night human, but if they were a bad night human. That might have made his opinion a bit different than most hunters.

"I'm actually not asking for me. I found another defecting hunter who wants to be rid of their night human side." Jax wasn't sure how much was safe to explain to Jo. She was still a hunter, after all. If he told the truth, he would be calling out her parents for lying to all of them.

"Sure," Jo drawled out with the slight accent she only used when she was being sarcastic.

"He's actually here for someone else," Beck came to his defense, which surprised Jax.

"There's another son that can stand to be around his

father? I wonder whose child that one is ..." Jo seemed to be seriously considering all her options.

Jax glanced at Beck. He wasn't sure how much Jo could be trusted, but it seemed his brother did. He had brought them to her for a reason. Beck gave a slight nod.

"Not a son, but a daughter," Jax explained. He reached for the water sitting in front of him.

Jo seemed shocked at that. "Jade wants to leave already? They haven't assigned her a mate yet."

Jax sputtered as he choked on the water he was drinking. Jade was only nineteen, nowhere near wanting to have a mate or anything like that. Heck, she hadn't really had time to date much with their mother's rigorous training schedule and insistence that Jade be a full hunter by eighteen. She didn't want kids, at least not right now. She had always talked about starting a family after she found the perfect man, like in decades.

"It's not Jade," Beck replied as he gave Jax a "did you just choke on water" look. Beck had all those looks down. Jax felt like he could never live up to his calm, collected brother.

"No way possible it's Jade. They're going to assign her a mate that soon?" Jax finally added what was bothering him.

"Actually, I'm surprised they haven't already. But if not Jade, then who?"

Jax didn't care what the hunters thought of Simone being alive, but he didn't want them to come searching. Not that it would do much good as his father was able to stay hidden from them, but something just made Jax want to protect her from it all. While they were family, they weren't trusted. He didn't know if they would make sure she was really dead if they knew what she planned to do.

"No one knows she's missing," Jax explained, getting back on track.

"It's a hunter everyone thinks is dead. She's sick and needs to be able to access her night human side to heal. That would make sense," Jo replied. "The barrier is the one thing that keeps us protected, but at the same time, it can bad for someone like your friend. We can't be turned into a night human, but then we can't use all the strengths and bonuses—such as the healing—like a night human either."

Jo nodded as she spoke like she was going through possible candidates for the person silently in her head, but Jax wasn't going to say anything further as to who she was no matter what Jo asked, or how close she came.

"Hunters don't get sick," Jo finally stated as she seemed to come to the end of her list of suspects.

Jax shrugged. What more could he say? He had been taught the same thing.

"She didn't get sick," Beck answered for Jax. "She was born sick and has been fighting it her whole life. She's losing and soon will be dead unless we can find out how to turn her."

Jo continued to nod as Beck spoke. "But you can't turn a hunter."

Beck now nodded. It was all what Jax already knew. Their cross-country drive was getting them nowhere.

"We aren't trying to turn her. If Wes thought it would work, he would have already done it. We need to release her night human side. Transform, not turn her."

"Can't be done," Jo replied again, steady in her answer. She leaned back and crossed her arms, daring the boys with her eyes to challenge her.

"I'm pretty sure it can," Beck answered back, calling her standoff. "Or I wouldn't be one."

"You don't count," Jo remarked as she leaned back to the table and picked up her drink. "You were never officially a hunter."

Beck shrugged. "My mother was a hunter, and my father was a night human. Neither I nor Devin changed when we came of age, so it must have been hidden just like every other hunter out there. But I'm one now. Something is different for me. There's a way for a hunter to change."

"You guys are a special case. I don't know if your mother sealed in your night human side since you were born outside the hunter clan."

"Sealed?" Jax caught the one word that gave Jo away. "What does that mean?" They had been speculating that it was something the hunters did, but now she confirmed it.

Jo blew out a deep breath, making her chop-job bangs blow up into the air.

"Okay. I understand that the night human side is sealed, but really, I can't help you. I know what everyone knows when they first join the hunters, but I never got far enough to see how it's done. I rejected the offer of a mate and chose to not have kids. So really, I can't help you." She held her hands up in surrender. Jax believed her, but he wondered if Beck did.

A loud crash at the bar made Jax turn around. Two night humans, one that looked like a walking fish face and one that had green goo coming out of his face, were now tangled together. The green goo was being flung everywhere. Blood would have been easier to see as Jax wanted to gag.

"While I wish I could help you, I can't, boys. And now our time is done. These things get rowdy if I don't stand at the bar to keep them in line."

Jo stood up, and Beck did the same. He offered a hand to JoJo and then grasped it, pulling her closer. He leaned down as she whispered in his ear, and he gave her a half hug, patting her on the back. There was something between them, and Jax was dying to know more that he would never learn. Beck rarely gave crucial information, and Jax knew he would never talk about his private life.

Jojo winked at Beck as she pulled back. "Take care of him, Beck. Jax is a good kid, and I'd hate for him to end up all boring like you." She ruffled Jax's hat as she pushed her way back through the crowd of night humans that had formed around the two fighting ones. Jax straightened his hat to keep his identity secret and followed Beck, who was already leaving through the now cleared area around the edge of the room. Hours and hours in the car had been for nothing after all.

CHAPTER 3

"**What a waste** of time," Jax complained as they made their way back out into the hot Arizona sun. Jax had lived in enough different parts of the US to be able to compare dry heat and humid heat, but in his book, the Arizona sun was its own classification.

Beck didn't reply as he led the way to the car. Jax followed behind, still not completely used to his silent brother. Jade was quiet around strangers, but alone, she was always talking. She would have been complaining with him. Jen, who Jax had just met when he arrived in New Orleans, was also a very talkative sister. Jax wasn't completely sure what to make of his silent sibling. Sometimes silence could be good, but Beck made Jax anxious.

"Watch out for scorpions and snakes," Beck said as he opened his car door.

Jax reached down to open his door and stopped as he looked inside. Leaving the top down on the convertible seemed to be an invitation to the snake that was now sunning itself in Jax's seat.

"Um, what do I do with it?" Jax asked. He wasn't sure what kind of snake it was. Was it poisonous?

"Move it," Beck replied like it was obvious.

Jax peered down at their visitor. It made no indication

that it noticed him.

"With what?"

Beck rolled his eyes at Jax. Without an answer, Beck moved at inhuman night human speed to grab the animal and toss it out the back of the car. The red-striped snake didn't have time to open its eyes. Jax was pretty sure that reptile had never been handled by a night human before.

"You need to stop thinking like a day human," Beck scolded Jax as he sat down. "Because you're not one anymore."

Jax wanted to object, but it was true. The thought to grab the snake and toss it never crossed his mind. Humans didn't go around picking up snakes if they didn't know what kind they were; it wasn't safe. Then again, most things that were once dangerous were probably not now with his father's blood still flowing in him. It was just that his body might have been temporarily changed into an invincible night human, but it didn't change the eighteen years he had been raised.

Beck didn't give the snake a second thought as he continued to scroll through his phone in the driver's seat. When he seemed to read enough, Beck tossed the phone into a neighboring convertible. Jax was pretty sure Beck wasn't ever without a phone. He had to answer their father at a moment's notice as well as be able to respond to the group he worked for hunting night humans.

"What?" Jax asked, confused as Beck started up the car and drove away from the run-down night human bar. He just left his phone behind without a care in the world.

Beck, as Mr. Silent, didn't explain as he drove back onto the main road. They hadn't gone far when Beck reached into his pocket to pull out a ringing phone. Did he have two phones? Jax couldn't be sure, but he hadn't noticed before. The best explanation Jax could think of was that the first phone had belonged to someone else and Jax only assumed it was Beck's, but that still didn't explain whose phone it was or why he had it.

"Did you get what you wanted off my phone?" a deep female voice asked. Jax did like his new super night human hearing. It took a moment, but he could place the voice as Jo's.

"Not too much in contact these days are you?" Beck countered.

At least now Jax understood whose phone Beck had. When he had taken it was still a mystery, and what he had been looking for was also, but since Beck wasn't going to explain, Jax would collect scraps of information as he could. He focused on their voices instead of the wind rushing by.

"I told you the truth—I can't help because I don't know. They don't tell these things to people who refuse their designated mate." Jo didn't sound mad at all that Beck stole her phone and went through it.

The trunk of the car thumped as Beck drove over a bump. Jax looked at the backseat. He didn't remember Beck packing anything in the trunk before they left, but then again, Beck could have had the trip planned for days before. Maybe he traveled with as many weapons as the hunters.

"Did you get my present?" Jo asked.

"Present?" Beck repeated.

There was another thump from the trunk, but this

time the car hadn't gone over any bumps. Jax glanced back and then at Beck again. He was positive they hadn't gone over anything to make that noise.

Beck pulled the car off to the side of the road, kicking up dirt all around them. Without saying anything more, he shut off his phone and tucked it back into his pocket. As he exited the car, Jax hurried out to stand beside his brother as he opened the trunk.

Jax didn't have time to duck as something shot out of the trunk straight at him. Caught off guard, Beck had to tackle Jax to the ground to keep him from getting hit. A half-snake man darted past them without a glance back. Beck's present?

Beck stood and dusted off his clothing before hopping back into the car without a word to Jax.

"What was that?" Jax asked as he got in, just as Beck was putting the car into gear.

"Obviously a night human," Beck replied. Jax wasn't sure, but he got the slight hint that Beck was upset. "One I've been hunting for over six months now."

"Oh." Jax didn't really have another reply. If he had been hunting a particular night human for six months, he would surely be mad if he lost it again. Maybe they did have more in common than Jax thought.

"You're welcome," Beck added as he whipped the car around and began driving in a new direction. "One bite from a serpentine is deadly to anyone with day human blood. Without a night human side, you would have been dead in minutes."

"Serpentine?" Jax had never heard of one before.

"They're like naga; it's just that all serpentine are

evil."

Jax nodded like he understood. Basically, an evil night human that could have killed him had just jumped out of the trunk of his brother's car after they had spent almost twenty-four hours straight driving. It made no sense and didn't seem possible.

"What do we do now?" Jax wondered if his brother would actually answer.

"Go hunting, what else?"

With one hand on the wheel and the wind whipping through his hair, Beck smiled at Jax. Any anger seemed forgotten. Beck was in his element, and Jax simply nodded. He wasn't sure he wanted to hunt something that could kill him easily, but he was certain that they couldn't let something like that roam around normal unsuspecting humans. Hunting it was then.

Beck drove for over an hour as Jax waited for him to explain something, anything. Jax had no idea what a serpentine was or how to fight or track it. And it wasn't like they were tracking. The creature had taken off into the desert, and they were driving along a road to somewhere. A sign indicating they were only twelve miles from a town flew past. That meant Jax had only ten minutes to get anything out of Beck.

"Are we heading to town to get supplies to track the target?"

Beck didn't even glance at him. "We're night humans, what supplies would we need? My bare hands seem in working order."

Jax didn't want to play the "answer with a question" game. Beck was good at that one. He was always trying to get him to think more, but really, Jax had no clue how to be a good night human. It was a side of him he wasn't sure he wanted to explore. Sure, he told their father he would stay, but he still wasn't certain if he actually wanted to be a full-time night human. Thanks to the hunters, he hadn't had to worry until now with Simone.

"Okay, fine. We don't need supplies." Jax guessed that was the answer Beck was looking for. "Why are we heading to a town and not chasing the snake man in the desert?"

"Do you like to walk around in deserts in the middle of the day? I can turn around and take you back, and you can do just that, or we can head to the only place that thing will go." Beck shrugged like he didn't care which way they chased the snake man.

"Why is this town the only place you're looking?" Jax really needed a guidebook to night humans, or maybe just one for Beck in particular.

"Serpentine don't use their snake form unless they're hungry, like need food now hunger. He had two options: head back to the bar where he was most likely captured, or head to the nearest town. This happens to be the nearest town, and I'm sure he's here."

Jax was still confused. How did Beck know it was the nearest town? As far as he'd seen, Jax had yet to see Beck look at a map. Maybe his brother had grown up in the area. At least that's what Jax was going to go with.

"What is the plan then? Do we just walk into town and the snake will come crawling back to you? Or do we wait to see what he's killed and track him that way?" Jax wasn't a fan of the second option, but he also didn't know how else to find the snake guy.

"We have to find him before he kills. After that, he will be just as normal as you are when you don't have father's blood in you. He will disappear again. That's why I can't seem to catch him. He's too good at being human."

They approached the edge of town. Jax could see houses clumped closer together, and soon enough they were driving down the main street. Shops and diners stood side-to-side in older brick buildings. It was as small-town America as you could get. Beck pulled off to park on a side street. When he got out of the car, Jax followed.

"How do we track him?" Jax hoped his brother put something on the snake as he tackled him. That would make perfect sense as to why Beck wasn't concerned about searching for him.

Beck looked at Jax like he could read his mind and he knew how crazy he was thinking.

"You track all the time," Beck replied like that was an answer. Yes, Jax tracked night humans, but they were ones he knew how to track. They left signs and almost always they were following a trail of dead bodies. According to Beck, that wasn't an option.

"Humor me," Jax responded.

"Do you know what your biggest problem is?" Beck asked, going back to giving a question as a reply and never giving a straight answer. Jax didn't know what to say. Like it mattered. Beck was probably just going to walk away and not tell him anyway.

Jax walked to the corner of the street they parked on. He could see the shops and people inside. Everyone was walking around as if it were a normal day. How they could find a blood-hungry leech in the town was beyond Jax. He wasn't sure what sort of trail you followed on a serpentine. Did he leave a sand trail like normal snakes? Would they need to circle the town to find how he entered? He had never heard of one before, and his night human lessons were quite thorough. Jax had to wonder if it was all a set-up. Maybe JoAnn and Beck thought it would be fun to tease him. That had to be it.

"You still think you're a human," Beck said as he stopped beside Jax. "That," Beck pinged Jax on his covered forehead, "proves you aren't just a human, but the brain inside your head can't seem to stop thinking that way."

"Forgetting eighteen years of being alive in a matter of weeks isn't possible. I can't simply ignore every instinct that has been put in me since I was little." And that was the truth. It wasn't a problem of wanting to be a night human or not. He was raised a day human, and it was going to take much longer to change that.

Beck shrugged. "I'm not asking you to not be a hunter. I'm telling you to actually follow your instincts. Long before you ever knew about me or our father, you knew there was something different about you. You could feel night humans. Not many hunters can do that. Could Jade?"

Jax didn't answer. Beck already knew what it would be. Jade couldn't feel night humans, and she couldn't tell the good ones from the bad ones. Only Jax could do that. But that didn't mean he knew how to be a night human. He was a day human and had been his whole life. That much didn't change.

"Now you need to use that side of you and help me find this thing before it disappears again."

Something in his voice made Jax stare at Beck. It was like he expected him to be able to just turn on that side. Jax had spent years hiding that much about him as it was strange to be different from the other hunters. Only his mother and sister knew he used his ability to tell who was a night human as often as he did.

Beck seemed to understand that Jax wasn't just able to do something magical as he finally continued talking.

"Okay. You are a touch type for sensing night humans. Have you ever tried using a different sense to do it?"

"Like looking at people? Because no, I can't tell by looking at someone if they're a night human," Jax replied. He had tried that more than a dozen times because he hated the feeling of touching the bad night humans. It was something he couldn't describe, but it made his skin crawl.

"I was thinking of a different sense." Closing his eyes, Beck took a deep breath.

"Like smelling them? What? Are we part dog also?" Jax tried to joke.

Beck didn't open his eyes as he stood completely still. After a moment, he turned and walked back toward the car. Jax scrambled to follow. Was it really that easy for Beck to track?

"So he didn't come here after all?" Jax guessed.

"Oh, no. The serpentine is here, but unless you stop him, he's going to kill innocent humans again."

Beck went to the front of the car and opened his door. Jax stayed by the back of the car in shock. Beck wasn't tracking the monster but letting it go. Seems the bloodsuckers did look after each other after all, no matter all the good guys and bad guys talk that Beck did.

"Wait. You want me to stop him? I thought one bite would kill me. And since I can't track him, wouldn't it be better if you did all that. Isn't it your job?"

"My job is to keep you safe, not humans," Beck replied as he slid into the front seat.

Jax stared at his brother. He was actually going to leave the monster running around a poor town that just happened to be close by. Someone was going to die at the hands of a half-snake monster, and Beck didn't care.

"I only know how to find night humans by touch if I go around touching them. I'm pretty sure snake man isn't going to wait around for that, and I'm pretty sure I don't need to touch him to know what he is. I'm not a night human like you. I don't have night human powers."

"But that's exactly what you keep ignoring. You are a night human. Right now with father's blood, you are a full night human. No partial crap. You have the same abilities as me and probably even better ones if you gave them a chance. Stop being afraid of this side of you, or someone is going to die."

Jax wanted to stand there and pout. He knew exactly what Beck was doing. He was playing on his very human side of wanting to protect the humans around him from the monsters. But he was forcing him to be a monster to do that. He wasn't sure it was a fair trade.

"Fine. How do I know what I'm smelling for?"

Jax gave in even though he wanted to protest more. His sensible side won. Whoever the snake was going to attack didn't have time for him to fight with Beck.

The trunk of the car popped open in front of Jax. It was completely empty. Beck traveled with nothing, which wasn't a surprise. Not even a weapon, but then again, his older brother was a weapon in itself.

"What do you smell?" Beck asked as he now stood beside Jax.

Jax shrugged. It was a dirty car that had been driving through deserts. It smelled like dirt.

"Take a deep breath and make mental notes of everything you can tell what it is."

He looked at Beck, trying to give him his best "are you kidding me" glare. However, he didn't have time as he found his face instantly pushed into the open trunk by Beck. Jax couldn't wait to be as strong and quick as his older brother.

"A real breath," Beck ordered, holding Jax in place.

Jax knew it was fruitless to argue with Beck. He took a deep breath and did his best to try to think of what everything was: dirt, flowers, plants, carpet, oil, car smells like rubber from the tires, and something that was just … off.

"What does the serpentine smell like?" Beck asked from behind him.

Jax glared at Beck when he released him, and Jax could finally stand straight, looking his older brother eye-to-eye. He didn't appreciate being manhandled.

"Ashes."

Beck smiled. "Sweet ashes. Every night human out there that is bad or has done bad stuff smells like ashes, but each should still smell distinct. The serpentine smells like sweet ashes."

"Okay. I can smell him in the trunk, but we knew he was in there for probably an hour or more. How do you find his scent out here?" There was much ground to cover, and Jax was sure they wouldn't make it in time.

"By taking a deep breath and knowing where to hunt it," Beck replied as he shut the trunk and walked back to the main street. "Time to practice those night human senses, little brother."

Jax took what seemed like his twentieth breath in less than a minute. He was honestly surprised he wasn't hyperventilating from it. It was harder now where they were standing. Beck didn't want them out in the open since they were closer to the serpentine, but standing by a tree was messing with everything for Jax. All he could smell were the leaves on the tree. Leaves had an actual smell, and Jax wasn't sure he would ever get over that. In fact, everything had a smell. And the serpentine wasn't the only night human in the city. Luckily, he was the evilest and thus smelled the strongest, but Beck had to keep Jax on track more than once as they made their way into the quiet streets of houses. There were a lot more night humans around than he ever suspected.

"Why do they always end up going into these nice

neighborhoods?" Jax complained, not expecting an answer.

He had noticed that immediately when he started hunting years ago. The night humans would have an easier time hiding in the bad parts of town where bodies were more common, but again and again night humans went to the nice middle-class neighborhoods and turned their lives into terror. They were always easy to track when they brought devastation to quiet little neighborhoods across the country.

"Because the food is better," Beck stated like it was obvious. "Now concentrate and find this guy before someone becomes his lunch."

"Or two someones," Jax added. He was pretty sure the flower smell mixing with the night human had to be a perfume. It wasn't the same scent as the flowers growing around town, and unless it was an exotic gardener, he was pretty sure it wasn't a kind grown in any garden in the state.

"Yes, I think you're right," Beck answered as he stood and peeked around the side of the tree. "How do you plan to take him down?"

Jax tried to keep his eyes from bugging. He thought the whole "follow your instinct and be a night human" part was done. The serpentine was deadly for him because no matter how much Beck wanted him to be a night human, and Jax was still part day human.

"Isn't it your job to protect me?"

"Yes, but it isn't my job to protect normal day humans. They aren't our equals. They are food for us." That was a shock for Jax to hear coming out of Beck's mouth.

"Then why do you hunt the bad night humans?" Jax hadn't meant to say it out loud, but it was true. If Beck didn't care about humans, then why hunt night humans?

"Because if we let the bad night humans have their way, there will be no food left for the rest of us. There needs to be a balance, and that's what I do."

Jax ignored his heartless night human brother. He had come to expect night humans caring very little for human life, but it was hard to hear it said so harshly from Beck. Beck still understood and remembered how it was to be human. Jax had thought that maybe his brother was helping keep humans safe because of what he went through himself, but he wasn't. Beck was just like the rest. And it was everything Jax didn't want to become.

Two houses down and across the street were an older couple watching TV in their house. It wasn't just that Jax could smell them along with the night human snake man hiding outside their house; he could hear the TV, too. The snake was outside, probably planning his move to get at his food without being caught. Jax figured if he could smell it, then couldn't it smell him? He had no idea how you could sneak up on it to capture him before he harmed the people.

"The snake guy is outside the window on the back of the house. I don't know if that's how he plans to go in. We can't see him from here, but I know he's there. My only question is that if night humans can sense each other, how do you sneak up on one?"

Beck smiled from beside Jax. With the night human blood of his father still running inside of him, Jax could see the subtle change in his brother. His face was no longer quite as beautiful as it was before. His hair was a fraction shorter and less glowing blond, and instead more of a dishwater-blond color. And his bright blue eyes were now flecked with gray.

"Best part of being a vampyre. I can turn it off as well as he can. Unfortunately, I don't change in appearance enough to be hidden, so he'll still run from me once he spots me because he knows who I am."

"Yay for you, but what about me?" Jax couldn't just turn it off. His father's blood was making his night human side present until it wore off and that would be at least another four or five hours away.

"Stay upwind, and you should be fine."

"You're not coming with me?"

Beck had told him a hundred times that he was there to protect him, but leaving him alone with a monster that could kill him didn't seem to be protecting. It wasn't like Beck to flake on his job.

"Nah. You should be fine. Actually, he probably won't consider using his poison. Right now he'll think you're a night human, so he's not likely to poison you. He wants to save it for the humans he plans to eat."

"Anything else you want to tell me?" Jax was dumbfounded that Beck was so relaxed about everything. Jax didn't know the slightest thing about a serpentine. Were they good fighters? Did they like close combat or to stay far away? What sort of weapons did they carry or have on them? Was their skin thick or thin? Was there a kill spot on them? Basically, everything Jax would find comforting to know, he didn't have a clue about.

"Nope, you should be fine. Good luck saving those humans because the serpentine aren't really known for patience. I doubt he'll sit there long." Beck moved over the stone fence at the house they were near and sat down.

If Beck was trying to get Jax to miss his sister, he was doing a good job. He hadn't missed her nearly as much as he did right now. And he kind of missed the other hunters, too. The way he was raised made him doubt attacking an unknown night human was a good idea, but what choice did he have? Those people were counting on him to save them, even if they didn't know he existed. As messed up as the hunter way of raising kids was, they were at least reliable and were always willing to lay their life down for the humans.

Jax reached up into the air and waited to feel the wind. Stay downwind was Beck's only helpful suggestion, but it was something Jax was sure he would have done anyways. He didn't have any weapons on him, but his weeks of training with Beck made it that he didn't need weapons now when he was in his father's form. His long claws, which grew on will, would be enough of a weapon. Jax took one last look at Beck, who seemed to be busy on his phone, and that was sufficient to make him determined to show his brother that he was good enough to get the slimy snake. Without another glance, Jax took to the shadows and made his way around the house where the snake man waited. He might not have been as good as Beck at staying hidden, but he was better than most. Hopefully, it would be enough.

"They really don't teach you much, or maybe your

mentor just stinks. Sorry, you got paired with such a lousy night hunter, kid," the snake man said. "Beck's been chasing me for close to five years. I almost feel bad having to do this."

Jax wasn't out of his hiding spot before he felt something wrap around his leg. He looked down in time to see the slithering appendage pull, and he went crashing into the sidewalk beside the snake man. Before he even had a chance to move, snake man already had another coil of tail around Jax's neck. It seemed that while he had a snake tail that was used to pull Jax from his spot, the snake man could also make his fingers into retractable snake appendages. Info like that would have been helpful.

"How did you know I was there?" Jax asked with the little breath he had left.

The snake man flickered out a tongue.

"My sense of taste is way better than smell, and wind doesn't affect me." Again, more that would have been good to know.

Jax felt the tentacle tighten around his throat. The snake's red eyes watched as Jax gasped for his last breaths while snake man smiled, showing his fangs. Jax felt the life draining from him as the snake man let go. The serpentine turned in what seemed like slow motion. His head fell from his body.

"What the ..." Jax said as he stood and wiped the brownish goo from his face—the insides of the snake man that were now all over him.

"Did you pee yourself?" Beck asked with a slight grin.

Jax didn't reply. He looked like he had showered in

the snake guy's blood.

"You were really just going to let me get killed," Jax complained as he wiped most of the goo off his face with the only clean part of his sleeve. Now he was completely covered.

"You weren't in any danger of dying. If you had been, you would have had a vision, and you would have told me," Beck pointed out.

Jax hadn't thought of that. Since he had been with his father, there hadn't been a single time he had had a vision about his life ending. His magic "see the future" power had saved him more than once since he had been in New Orleans, but Beck was right. There was no vision now. Originally Jax thought that maybe being with the vampyre made them go away, but he suspected that they were gone because he was safe all the time. No one was going to attack him with who his father was.

"Maybe it doesn't work with night human blood in me," Jax suggested. It really felt like his life was on the line.

"There's always been night human blood in you," Beck pointed out as he easily transformed back into his night human form before picking up the body of the dead serpentine. "Can you get his head?"

Jax reached down and picked up the severed head by the black ponytail hanging off the back of it. His eyes were still open, but no longer glowing.

"Don't touch his fangs. They can still kill you," Beck told him as they made their way back around the house. Beck didn't attempt to hide the fact that he was carrying a body down the sidewalk as they made their way back to the car.

"So why do you need to stay around to protect me if I have this gift that didn't seem to work this time?" Jax inquired as they walked. It was just a thought, but one that now made him wonder. Why did Beck have to be around protecting him if Jax had the means to protect himself?

"Are you dead?"

"No."

"Then your powers still work."

Beck was done with that conversation, but Jax wasn't.

"That doesn't answer the question," Jax pointed out as they made it to the car.

Beck popped the trunk and tossed the body inside. Jax glared at Beck, waiting for his answer. Beck motioned for Jax to add the head. Jax dropped it inside the trunk, being careful not to touch the mouth of the creature. He still didn't have his answer.

"Your power is to protect you when there isn't an alternative way to do something."

"That makes no sense. There's an alternative to everything."

After shutting the trunk, Beck turned to find a girl on a bike watching them. Jax waited for to her scream and run away. She had to see that they had just carried a body and tossed it into their car.

"Hey, sweetie," Beck called to the girl. She stayed frozen on her bike. "You won't remember seeing anyone here today. In fact, it's getting pretty late, so you're going to head home and tell your parents that you had a fun time riding today."

"Yes." The girl nodded. "I had a fun time riding my bike."

Without a second glance at them, she turned her bike around and left.

"Sometimes in life, no matter how many chances you get, you won't be able to save everyone. I'm here for the moment you can't be saved. Like if you accidentally touched that fang."

"Wouldn't I just go back and know not to do it?"

"Possibly, or possibly you would go back and do it again. Father doesn't want to take the chance. We aren't sure how that power works. You are too valuable to him." Beck went to the front of the car and slid into the driver's seat.

"Not in hunter form," Jax muttered under his breath as he got back inside the car with his brother.

"That's true also. Jo's phone didn't give me any clues. She really isn't in touch with the hunters. We'll have to head home and try another route. I'm sure Wes is waiting. We just have to keep looking on our own. It's got to be something all hunters have in common."

Beck reached to the back seat and pulled out a towel that he handed to Jax before starting up the car to leave. Jax wiped off the rest of his face to be sure it was clean of the snake blood and then moved onto his arms. Stopping at the tattoo on his forearm, Jax had to wonder. All hunters were marked with the same tattoo. Was the magic seal in it?

CHAPTER 4

Jax wasn't completely sure, but it didn't seem that they were heading back the same way they came. Okay, he was sure they weren't. He could tell, like any good hunter, that they weren't traveling east, but more northeast. Also, since Beck had turned off on roads, it was a sign they were taking a different route home. The way there had been one highway the whole time. They didn't exit or go on any other road. They weren't on that highway anymore.

Jax didn't ask any questions because Beck was sure to not answer them. Perhaps Beck had more leads to follow, or maybe it was just a joy ride for his brother. He really didn't know what it was with that guy. Yes, they were blood-related, but there wasn't much else between them that was similar.

When Beck drove into a town beyond the gas station, Jax knew that Beck wasn't taking them home yet and he had to wonder what was coming next. He drove down the main street and took a turn into a more industrial side of town, wherever they were. After a few more minutes of driving, Beck pulled up to a factory so run-down that Jax couldn't even read what was formerly written on the outside of the building.

Beck hopped out of the car and opened the trunk.

"Take the head, would you?"

Jax wasn't sure what they were doing now, but he followed behind Beck with the head of the dead snake guy. He was happy to see the car ride had closed the head's mouth. Jax didn't know how long the fangs would remain poisonous.

Without hesitating, Beck walked into the old building with a headless man in his arms. Jax hoped it was as deserted in the inside as it appeared on the outside, because otherwise they would have a lot of explaining to do.

After pushing open the door with his feet just like Beck had, Jax found Beck standing at a counter-like reception wall with a solid black glass window. There was a small hole that Beck was sticking his hand through as he balanced the dead body against his shoulder with just one arm.

"Enter, Captain," a robotic voice said from behind the opaque wall. Beck pulled his arm back, but not quick enough for Jax to see the blood beading up on it. Something had just cut Beck.

"Captain?" Jax finally spoke. Beck turned and nodded to Jax.

A buzz sounded before the insanely thick door next to the reception wall opened up with a slow cranking noise. Beck just stood and waited, and Jax followed suit. When the door was all the way open, Beck walked into what appeared to be a solid metal box. Jax wasn't claustrophobic, but this space was strange enough to make him become it soon.

"Come on," Beck grumbled to Jax, who stood outside

the box looking in.

Jax moved forward with snake-man's head. While it was tempting to just toss the head inside with Beck, he had a feeling it wasn't going to be that easy. Beck acted like nothing was going on, but Jax had seen more than once that his brother never really took his eyes off of him, probably an order from their father.

As the door cranked shut, Jax realized there was no light in the box. And for that matter, no fresh air either. With the last clank, the box basically sealed them inside complete blackness with a dead corpse that might not be rotting yet, but would soon. Jax sure hoped Beck knew what he was doing as he stood still and didn't move. The snake head was potentially life-threatening to Jax. He wasn't going to move a muscle as they waited for whatever was coming next.

While they stood there, Jax expected Beck to explain, but of course, his older brother was tight-lipped as ever. Jax considered humming a tune to pass the time and hopefully annoy Beck, but he didn't need to as the door clanked and began to open again. Jax wasn't sure what to think as soon as the doorway opened the full distance. They were no longer looking into the empty front room they had just left. They were in a clean hallway, nothing like the dilapidated room above.

"Move," Beck ordered, and Jax walked forward, finally noticing the small crease in the floor he had stepped over before. The metal box seemed to be a sort of elevator.

Beck walked by, dripping goo onto the floor from the severed neck. He didn't even glance back to see that he was making a mess or to check that Jax was following. Jax hurried to keep up with him. As they neared the end of the hallway, Beck kicked out a foot to hit a lever about knee high that caused the shiny steel double doors in front of him to open. Jax stood in shock as he peered into a large room. Heck, it couldn't be called a room. It was bigger than some airplane hangars Jax had been in, but it was filled from floor to the ceiling—at least four floors up—with shelves and boxes. It was a huge storage area.

"I have target 3252," Beck told someone. Jax turned to see that his brother hadn't walked into the hangar but had stopped at the entrance. Someone came from out of view with a gurney and a box. Beck dropped the body into the box and turned to Jax.

"Just toss the head in," he told him. Jax didn't toss but lightly placed the snake man's head in the box with the rest of him. A grayish-colored man nodded to Beck and rolled the body away, down one of the very long rows containing the same rustic-looking boxes.

Beck turned and went back to the hallway without a single explanation.

"Where are we?" Jax had to ask.

"At one of our chop shops," Beck answered. "Every target has to be dropped off at a shop that catalogs the kill and makes sure we had the right target. We don't have a fancy cleanup crew like the hunters. We have to clean up after ourselves."

Jax gaped at the rows of boxes. He didn't want to ask what would be done if it was the wrong kill. He had a feeling Beck didn't make mistakes. The room behind them was filled. The hunters were prolific in their kills, but if this was just one place for the night hunters to drop off their trophies, Jax had a feeling that the night hunters were a bit more prolific than his own day human clan had ever been.

Beck led Jax back upstairs to the car and drove off without any further explanation. Jax was still in shock by what he had just seen. He had pictured Beck's hunters more often just stepping in every now and then. Clearly, though, it was a lot more than now and then. It kind of made Jax feel like the hunters he had grown up in just didn't compare. Then again, he found most people— night or day human alike—didn't compare to Beck. And that was a lot to live up to.

Unfortunately for Jax, Beck was his older brother. He'd probably spend his life trying to live up to him, and for some reason, Jax was pretty sure Beck would always be one step ahead. Jax wished his night human superpower was to suck info out of people and he could speed up the whole training process by just touching them. Maybe then he could keep up with Beck.

When Beck didn't leave town, but made his way to a fancy hotel, Jax finally found his voice again.

"I thought all great night humans didn't sleep?"

Jax didn't just think that. He knew. Their drive to Arizona had been straight through, never stopping to rest or sleep. Beck was like a robot. In fact, Jax hadn't ever even seen him feed either. He was one strange night human.

Beck just shook his head as he parked the car and got

out. Another unanswered question.

Jax followed behind him, not sure what they were up to, yet again. That was becoming the theme in their relationship. It would have been nice if it could change, but Jax was more than sure Beck was like an old dog and lived by the saying "you can't teach an old dog new tricks". Beck waved to the front desk lady and walked right by without asking for a room. Heading to the elevator, he pulled a card out of his pocket. He put it in and pushed the button for the top floor. At least this time Jax knew he was in an elevator. That steel box at the chop shop had been beyond creepy.

As the elevator door pinged and opened, Jax realized the top floor wasn't a hallway to rooms but an actual room—the penthouse suite.

Inside was a lavish open floor plan with sitting areas to the left and right, and windows that lined the walls giving the best views. If it wasn't for the elevator, they were in and the wall in front of them, it would actually be a 360-degree view. Beck didn't take a moment before walking to the right and into a door beside the elevator. Jax really didn't need another elevator ride, but he followed behind, pausing when he realized he was walking into a corner meeting room filled with night humans. Seven extremely large men sat around, waiting.

"I'm glad you could all meet on short notice," Beck said as he entered the room. He was the smallest of the bunch.

Jax stood behind him in awe. He could feel the power radiating off the men. Normally he had to touch someone, but that wasn't needed here. These men were strong. Beck ignored Jax and went over to the seat at the head of the table to sit down. There weren't any seats left, and Jax was pretty sure he hadn't been invited to the party anyway, so he just wandered back out of the room.

"Don't leave this floor," Beck told Jax as he left. Jax gave him a wave without turning around.

Beck was inside talking with the various people. It sounded like they were all giving him reports of their activity or debriefing about the night humans they were tracking. It wasn't anything Jax needed to know or care about. He had one mission, and that was to remove the hunter seal on his night human side to save Simone.

Jax wandered to the left side of the elevator and the open room there. Three large, white couches were arranged for people to sit facing each other. White wasn't a color Jax was used to. In fact, the whole lavish hotel and penthouse suite was a bit odd, too. Hunters were always dirty and needed to blend in. They stayed at the cheapest and filthiest places. Jax was pretty sure the hotels for hunters were never above two stars at the most. Hunting didn't pay much, and they would have ruined a room like this in minutes coming back from a kill. Jax didn't blend in in the night human world, but Beck did. Maybe that was why he fit with the vampyre life much more easily than Jax did. Their father had money and stayed in places like the posh suite they were in now all the time.

Jax stared out the window to the open city below him. Having no clue where he was, Jax looked for some sort of marker or part of the landscape that would help. There was nothing. He wasn't sure where he was or when they were leaving. He could have paid more attention on the ride, but he kind of figured it didn't matter. It wasn't like Beck was going to let him drive his car. It was his baby.

Jax turned to go back and see what Beck was up to. He was finished waiting around in a place that made him uncomfortable. They were supposed to be searching for clues to help Simone, and Beck wasn't doing that. It wasn't like Jax was just going to lie around and wait. They needed to get back and speak with their father. They wanted to go on their next search. And for that Jax needed Beck. Jax walked back toward the meeting room.

Actually, it seemed that he didn't need his brother to get back. The car keys were sitting right beside the elevator door on a table. Jax forgot that Beck had set them down. Jax would have to keep his phone off to keep Beck from tracking him, but the first gas station he could find would be enough for Jax to figure out his way home. He had a credit card from their dad. It would be fine. Jax reached up to push the button on the elevator with one hand while swiping the keys with the other.

"I wouldn't do that," a female voice said from the room he had just been in.

Jax turned to find a raven-haired, petite woman sitting on one of the white lush couches.

"Beck would be upset with you, and I'm sure you know when he's upset you end up with a few more bruises when training since he can't touch you otherwise," she explained. Jax knew that, but how did she?

Gracefully, she stood up and offered Jax her hand.

"I'm Mei, Beck's better half," she introduced herself.

Jax just stared at her in shock. He hadn't thought about Beck having a girlfriend. He took her hand as he realized she still held it there for him to shake. He felt the rush of warm feelings indicating she was a night human, but a safe one. Taking her hand back, she smiled.

"I didn't know—"

Mei smiled. "The vampyre don't know. As far as your father is concerned, I'm just one of Beck's people, not his mate. We'd prefer to keep it that way."

Raising an eyebrow, Jax was at a loss as to what to say. He thought Beck was the perfect son, doing everything and anything Wes asked of him. Having a mate without their father's knowledge was out of character for Beck.

Mei patted the couch where she sat down, indicating that Jax should join her. He stumbled over and landed next to her. He wasn't sure what kind of night human she was, but like Beck, she seemed more human than anything.

"Long day?" she asked. "I bet he drove the whole time and didn't even let you break to pee."

Jax nodded. That pretty much summed up their day beyond the not getting any useful information.

"Typical Beck. Sorry about that. He's very mission-orientated. That's why they made him a captain of his own crew. But it does make him a pain to travel with." Mei smiled at Jax, and he was still not processing what to say. "I know from experience and can feel for you."

Beck had seemed, from the first moment Jax met him, like a loner type. He didn't need anyone else, and he surely didn't want anyone else. The guy barely talked. To know that he had a mate waiting back for him was beyond comprehension. Maybe she was just playing a joke on Jax. That had to be it.

Mei waited for Jax to speak further.

"How long have you been together?" Jax asked casually, waiting to see where she'd slip up if she was just playing a prank.

"About ten years. We were on a three-person team to hunt down a night human when we decided we'd rather be a two-person team," she explained, a slight blush creeping into her cheeks.

Plausible, but that could also be made up.

"How's Simone doing?" Mei asked. Jax sucked in his breath. First, she had mentioned how Beck was harder training him when he was mad, and now Simone. If she was playing a joke on him, she was really good.

"Not well and this trip didn't help. We are no closer than we had been before we left."

"I'm sorry this is so hard for you. I know how much it means to Wes to have you, and let me tell you, I'm happy you finally went to see him. I worry so much less about Beck when I know he's in New Orleans rather than following around the hunters. Your mother is kind of crazy in hunter terms—night or day human hunters. No offense," she quickly added.

"None taken," Jax replied. Really, his mother was well-known for all her crazy stunts and kills. "This isn't a joke, is it?" Jax finally blurted out. Mei seemed so genuine and nice.

"What?"

"You and Beck. You are really his mate."

Mei laughed. "I get it. The Beck you see isn't the one I get to have. Just wait for the guys to leave. I'll show you this is real. I'm Beck's mate."

And as if on cue, the night humans in the meeting room were all walking to the elevator. Beck followed them and waited for the door to close before he turned around with a big grin on his face. Mei jumped up from the sofa and ran into his arms. Beck lifted the tiny night human off the ground as she wrapped her legs around his waist like she was going to do a takedown move, but instead, Jax watched as she pressed her lips to Beck's. Jax turned away. He didn't need to see his older brother making out with his mate. They really were bonded. Go figure. Perfect Beck had a secret from dear old Dad.

"Sorry," Mei said quietly as they came back over to the couches and sat down. "We haven't seen each other in over a week."

Jax was going to guess months, not a week with that kind of welcome.

"She can't come around the vampyre too often, or Wes will suspect the truth," Beck explained as Mei curled into his arms. "I only block one thing from Wes mentally, so he's never suspected or gone looking through my mind. If he thinks I'm hiding something from him, he won't stop until he finds it."

"Well, that's something you'll have to teach me."

Jax really could use keeping his mind his own from his father. That was the one thing about being a night human that drove him nuts. Because his father was the leader, he had twenty-four-seven access to Jax's mind. It would be nice to have something be his own again.

"And why can't he know?" Jax added. What difference did it make if Beck had a mate? If their father knew, then maybe they wouldn't have to stay apart.

"I've seen his plans. He wants to grow the family by blood relatives, not the kind he makes by killing them; especially after how he was betrayed this time. It was a lot to lose at one time. He thinks if we start having children, we can create a new line in the family that can rule over the rest of the vampyre."

Making new little vampyre wasn't on his to-do list, but Jax could understand it being on his father's. Wes Cunningham, no matter how charming, was still a night human. They only thought of one thing, and that was power. Jax would deal with that when it came to it, but for now, at least he could put it out of his mind.

"And what about me thinking of you two? Won't I give it away?" Jax didn't need to be their downfall.

Mei grinned. "Nope. When I shook your hand before I used my night human power to allow you to see me. You couldn't before and won't when you look back at your memories."

"So if I met you on the street ..."

"You'd never know."

Beck tucked her closer into his arms and kissed the top of her head. Mei looked up at him, and a peaceful smile passed on Beck's face. He wasn't just smiling; he was genuinely happy. If this was what finding your mate was like, Jax was hoping he'd find his own one day. Super serious Beck was gone, and someone else was in his place. She was right. This was a completely different side of him. He was more relaxed and actually talking and hugging. Really, Jax never pegged Beck as a hugger.

"You have to leave soon," Mei guessed.

Beck nodded and kissed the top of her head again. "I'd stay longer if we could, but Simone needs an answer soon. She's failing quicker than we thought she would."

Jax nodded as Beck stood and he followed. As much as Jax wanted to see more of the weird side of Beck, they needed to find a way to break the seal before it was too late. Simone only had so much time.

Mei threw herself one more time into Beck's arms before he hit the button for the elevator. Jax averted his gaze, not wanting to intrude. As Beck pulled back and stepped on the elevator, Mei offered Jax her hand. He took it.

"You won't remember me, but you'll remember Beck. Remember that you don't have to focus just on the mission. Yes, we might be night humans, but we are just that—human. Don't forget to be one, and don't be afraid to love and live. Tomorrow isn't promised, but don't forget about today."

Jax stepped on the elevator and took one last look at the room they had just been in. It was empty, and he couldn't figure out why. He could have sworn he had been talking to someone or thinking something. Now it all seemed lost. Beck stared into the room as the door shut. It was the expression on his face that made Jax feel like there was something more he was missing.

Beck drove in silence as they left wherever they had stopped. He hadn't smiled since the elevator door shut. Jax wasn't sure how often Beck checked in with his crew, but they were efficient and didn't take more than an hour off the trip, not including however far they went out of their drive to be there. Hunter meetings were never that quick at home.

When Jax finally couldn't take the silence, he turned to Beck.

"Captain?" he asked with a grin.

Beck reached over and pinged his ear before he could move away. Darn night human speed.

"Yes, I lead a crew. It's better than following orders," Beck replied.

Jax felt as though his memories were fuzzy. There was something else there, too. He hated to forget something.

"Did you drug me?" Jax didn't remember eating or drinking anything, but that didn't mean it couldn't be airborne.

"No. You just met another member of my crew who's good at making people forget."

Jax eyed Beck over. First off, he was being friendly and answering questions. Second, Jax wouldn't let himself forget. It was dangerous in the night human world to forget. That was one of the first lessons as a hunter: Never forget anything, even small details can mean the difference between surviving or not.

"And there's nothing to worry about. I was there the whole time."

That wasn't too reassuring.

"And we didn't experiment on you. She wouldn't let

me." Then Beck laughed.

Jax didn't know what to make of his serious older brother laughing. That wasn't something expected. In fact, up until this moment, Jax hadn't been sure Beck knew how to laugh, or even smile for that matter. Maybe his brother had been replaced by a shape-shifting night human version of him. But Jax had never heard of one like that, especially someone who could mimic the power emanating from Beck. Jax was pretty sure his brother was his brother.

"No, seriously. You were fine with forgetting; you even let her do it a second time."

If Jax let someone mess with his memories, there had to be a really good reason. He eyed Beck over. What was the reason?

"Did we come up with a new solution to try?"

Beck shook his head and his smile faded. "Jo wasn't as helpful as I had hoped. We'll have to go back and talk with Wes some more. Maybe he's found out something that could be useful."

Jax doubted that. If their father knew how to make him a night human full time, he was pretty sure he would have done it by now. It wasn't that Jax wasn't welcome with the vampyre, but he knew what his father wanted.

"So home and then …"

"We figure it out," Beck answered.

"And if we don't?"

"Then you sit and hold her hand as she passes on."

It wasn't the answer Jax expected or wanted to hear.

Beck glanced at Jax and continued. "One thing I learned when my family was taken from me is some things you don't have control over. Even if you try your hardest, you will fail. And you can't let that be the end of you. You have to keep going. And you have to value the people in the time you have. Life isn't a guarantee even when you're a night human. Our father has been alive for what seems like forever, but even he will be gone one day. The Firsts are almost all gone already. It will happen."

Staring out at the road, Jax refused to meet Beck's gaze. He wasn't going to give up. He couldn't. Simone needed help, and he was the only one who could do it. He was the only one that cared enough to do it.

"We don't give up now. We still have time," Beck added as Jax sulked, as if he was reading his mind.

"Not much," Jax replied, as he rolled up his coat and went to lay back his seat.

Simone was fading faster every day. There really wasn't going to be much time, and Jax needed to try everything he could think of as fast as he could. He peeked over at his brother. There wasn't a tattoo on Beck, but he had mentioned he had something before he died. If his mother was a hunter, she could have known how to keep his night human side at bay. It was probably in the mark he wore without knowing. They all wore one—that was the one thing in common. Jax needed time to sort it out, but it might just come down to trying it. He wasn't sure what his father would think, but the man was anxious to get Jax as a night human. Jax had to hope that was enough.

CHAPTER 5

Sitting in the garden next to Simone, Jax couldn't help but notice how frail she was getting. She had seemed in good spirits and health before he left—he had made sure of it—but now she seemed as sick as all her doctors' charts made her. He understood completely why her parents thought she'd die quickly. He was wondering himself if he was going to find her a cure in time.

"I'm not dead yet," Simone teased, like she was reading his mind.

"But you will be if we don't figure this out," Jax replied dejectedly. He couldn't hide his pain from her. She knew him too well.

Jax had hoped Beck's contact would prove helpful, but it hadn't been. Yes, they caught one of the night humans Beck was hunting in his free time—hooray for ridding the world of one more evil leech—but they were no closer to finding the reason hunters kept their night human sides at bay. Beck wasn't sure where to start. Jax had an idea, but he was pretty sure his father and brother weren't going to like it.

"Let's go over this all again," Simone suggested as she laid a feather-light hand on top of his hand. He didn't need night human sight to see the blood beneath her skin; she was pale enough that he could see the veins crisscrossing her hand with his human eyes.

"There isn't anything to go over. Something about us makes it, so we don't turn into night humans. JoAnn appeared to think it had something to do with how we're born, or our mate is chosen, or something, but she couldn't give any further details because she never did that. Beck seems to think it's something the hunters do to us. I don't know who's right, but we need to figure this out fast."

"Beck never turned, neither did his brother, right?" Simone was frail, but she was still alive, and her brain worked completely fine even if her body didn't.

"No. He only turned after his death. According to him, our brother is still a day human, so maybe it's something about how we're made." Jax was grasping for ideas.

"But you can't be certain it isn't something our parents did to us. Beck's mother was a hunter, whether she was in with the hunters or not. She chose to have a child with your father. Maybe she did something to him to keep his hunter side in control. She probably knew how to keep him safe. If only we could talk to her."

That would have been nice, but from the very little Jax knew about Beck, his family had been attacked by a night human when he was a teen. The night human drained his parents before killing him and then tried to kill his younger brother. His brother was saved and raised by a night human, and Beck, along with his mother and father, were buried. Beck never explained further, but since Jax had seen vampyre rise from the dead after being buried, he had an idea where the story went.

"But what do our parents do that's the same with all of us?"

Jax turned the conversation from Beck back to their problem. Beck had no clue why he was turned, and even though he didn't share a lot, Jax believed him. Jax let his eyes roam over Simone's right forearm where her tattoo matched his.

"Why do we all have the same tattoo?"

Simone studied Jax's tattoo as he hers. Some had bigger ones like Jade did, and actually, Simone's was a little bigger than Jax's also, but it was still the same design. Every twist and turn of the Celtic cross on her arm matched Jax's arm, and any arm of a hunter. Jax thought it was just a calling card to recognize other hunters, but what if it had more meaning? What if there was a spell on it or it was made with special spelled ink? Witches existed, and he had a feeling they were part of the hunter secret. They were the only other non-night humans who were part of the night human world that he knew about.

"But Beck doesn't have the cross," Simone added as she looked at their arms together.

"Mine goes away when I transform," Jax replied. "What if Beck had something there before? What if now that he's a vampyre it's gone completely?"

"I did have a mark there before, but it was so small I never knew what it was," Beck added as he appeared from nowhere behind them. "Miss Simone, I need to take you to treatment."

"Was it a cross?"

"I really don't know. It could have been. But you're

right. I haven't seen it since I transformed."

Beck held out a hand for Simone. She took it, and Jax watched as Beck did most of the work to pull her to standing. She didn't have the strength to go from sitting to standing. His eyes weren't failing him. She was very sick. And he was the key to helping her. He didn't have time to keep searching for other more practical options, and he didn't have time to question himself as to whether he wanted to be a night human or not.

"I'll see you tomorrow?" she asked.

"Yes, when you're feeling better," Jax replied as he rose and kissed her on the cheek. She blushed as Beck led her away.

Jax waited for her to be out of sight before he sat back down. He had a feeling his tattoo had something to do with his hunter night human conundrum, but he wasn't sure enough to ask to have Simone's removed. It was possible that it would heal her completely, but there was also the possibility it could weaken her enough that if it wasn't the answer, then it could cost her her life. The only thing Jax could do was to do it to himself first.

Jax looked around the garden to be sure he was alone. His night human blood was tempting to the night humans around that weren't the vampyre. Strangely enough, he found he could trust the vampyre. It probably was because they feared his father. After the last attempt on his life, it seemed they were one hundred percent loyal to the clan.

Slipping off his shirt, Jax wadded it up into a tight ball to bite down on. It wasn't going to be fun to skin his own arm, but he had to. Simone wasn't going to last much longer.

Without a second thought, Jax sliced into the skin around the tattoo, trying to only go deep enough to remove the skin. Blood gushed down his arm, but Jax kept his hand steady as he cut slowly. While he didn't care about scarring, he didn't want to lose too much blood. As he made his way around the outside edge, he grabbed it to start peeling back the skin. As much pain as he was in, he couldn't fail to notice the top of the tattoo was already knitting back together. Jax stopped to watch the skin that was moving on its own. He was going to have to cut deeper, but that risked losing too much blood. There was already a puddle at his feet. It was dangerous to have such blood loss for his own health, and anyone passing that wanted a taste. His wonderful night human healing abilities that he loved as a hunter were now a problem. He just needed a way around them. How could you skin a night human quickly without killing them? Jax nodded to himself. He knew exactly how, and it was time for another road trip. This time he would be calling the shots.

The ocean water was bumpy as his boat skipped along full speed, but Jax didn't mind. It was great to be meeting up with his friends. Jax had never had night human friends before Sam and Whitney. Actually, Whitney had been the first night human that he had recognized there was something different with her. It felt like she was a night human, but it was completely different than all the people he had hunted over the years. What Jax didn't know then was that he was starting to differentiate the good from the bad. Jax refused to tell his mother or sister that Whitney was a night human because he knew they would attack first and ask questions later, and he was more than glad he didn't tell them. Whitney was truly one of the good guys, no matter what type of human she was.

Beck didn't seem to like the boat ride. For being such a tough night human, he sure was sensitive to the waves. Jax hadn't invited him to come, but it seemed that where Jax went, his shadow of an older brother went also. Jax had a feeling Beck was a land person, not an ocean person. Secretly Jax was having more than a little fun seeing his brother had a weakness. Tough night human killing machine Beck was taken down a couple notches by waves.

The boat finally slowed down, and the captain came over to Jax.

"This is where we take you to shore." The man pointed over to the island that secretly held more than a few dead mer bodies the last time Jax had been there over six months ago. He had helped Whitney take out many of the bad mer as she turned the ocean into a peaceful place like it was always meant to be.

"Sounds great," Jax replied.

Beck looked skeptically at the small boat that was being lowered into the water. It was a standard size rowboat with a small motor attached. It wasn't what you'd want to be out in the ocean in, but it was just taking them to shore.

"What? Doesn't your kind swim?" Jax teased. Beck

responded by pushing Jax toward the edge of the boat.

"You first, little brother," Beck replied.

Jax smiled and didn't hesitate to climb down the ladder, jumping off into the boat before he made it all the way down. It rocked beneath his feet, but Jax didn't fear the water. Whitney was probably somewhere nearby, watching them. He could swim, but she'd never let him drown. Beck climbed down beside Jax. He hid his dislike of the situation well, and that was just irritating to Jax. Beck couldn't be perfect at everything, though it seemed it was possible.

"Not camping?" the guy steering the boat to shore asked as Jax and Beck had nothing with them.

"Meeting friends," Jax replied. "Since we came from out of town, we let them pack everything."

That seemed to be enough of a reply that the guy either took it or was nodding because he really didn't care. Jax had a feeling it was the latter. They had to be used to hauling people out to the island as Sam said it had been used for decades as a jumping point to the siren island.

Sam and Whitney were already waiting on the island right at the tree line. Sam's dark hair contrasted with Whitney's blond curls, which were being tousled in the wind. They were wearing only swimsuits as they waved to Jax, walking through the shallow water to the boat as it got closer.

"He can't really be your brother," Whitney commented as Jax hopped out of the boat with Beck right behind him.

"Half-brother," Jax replied.

"No Jade?" Sam asked as he led the way onto the sandy beach after thanking the boat captain and sending him back to the larger ship.

"No. She's a full-time hunter now, and I'm a ...." Jax wasn't sure what he was now.

"Too bad. I got this planned out so cool, I know that she would love it," Whitney replied, filling the awkward space Jax left. That was one of the great things about Whitney. Things were never awkward with her; she just didn't let it be.

Sam nodded. "She's been planning this since you called," he added.

Talking to Sam and Whitney was like talking to one person. They were complete opposites, with Sam's dark hair and dark personality and Whitney's blond sunshine that seemed to follow her everywhere she went. But somehow they were always on the exact same train of thought. Jax had to imagine it was the night human bond they shared. He had read about it in his training, but he had never thought much about it. Being close to being a night human, it was possible he would find that same bond someday. And that was a strange thought.

"I swear you look familiar," Whitney added as she looked around Jax at Beck. "Have we met before?"

"I've never met a siren. I knew there were some around, but even the night hunters weren't aware there were that many," Beck replied, swiping his hand through his perfectly messy hair. Yep, his hair was perfect.

"Oceanid," Sam replied.

"Oceanid?"

"I'm not a siren, it turns out," Whitney explained as

Sam kept them walking. They were now off the beach and starting down a path through the trees in the middle of the island.

"I don't know if I ever was a siren, but it's a long story." Whitney shrugged.

"Which you'll text me later?" Jax added. He loved her stories. They were always an adventure. He had met her last year when his hunter family had moved to Florida to search for a suspected mer. Mer were outlawed in the night human world. Whitney had accidentally become one when Sam saved her life with his blood. Her accidental luck was something Jax could use.

Whitney grinned. "Only if you share with Jade because she'll kill me if I tell you and not her. How's she doing?"

"Good, the last time I checked, but it's been weeks. She's grown a little bossy since she became a full-fledged hunter, but she's still Jade. I know my mother will keep her safe, or at least I hope she will since she only has one child left at home."

Jax shrugged. There really wasn't much more he could tell. Jade was forbidden from talking with night humans now unless she was hunting them, and Whitney would never be hunted. No matter that they were friends; she couldn't openly talk with Whitney now. The night human council had reinstated merfolk as long as they sported pink on their fins. Jax wasn't sure what that meant, but he was going to ask Whitney when he got the chance.

"You moved out? I thought you were joking."

Jax smiled at her shock. Whitney had met Rommy

and knew how intense the hunter was.

"Nope, no joke. I'm staying at my dad's place." Jax stepped under the low-hanging branch that Beck had just walked under behind Sam. Whitney and Jax were getting a little behind them as they talked.

"You found your dad?" she squealed in delight.

"Yeah, turns out he's a night human."

Whitney covered her mouth with her hands. Then she shook her blond curls. "No way. Then you'd be one."

And that was what everyone would think. Jax knew otherwise, but he was about to change it. He hadn't explained to Whitney why he needed the healing water beyond cutting off his tattoo. He wasn't sure she would be on board or not if she knew what he was really doing. His mother was a very fearsome person, and Jax was positive Whitney would never intentionally get on her bad side.

"All hunters come from a hunter female and a night human male," Jax explained how he came to be.

Whitney nodded like that could make sense. It didn't, but she was nice enough to not question more. She turned to find Sam and Beck far ahead.

"Oops," she said as she began to jog to catch up with them. Jax kept pace behind her.

"I'm just happy Jax didn't bring his mother. My dad is still mad at me that she helped with our last mess of cleaning up the mer," Sam was explaining to Beck.

"Your father doesn't like hunters? That makes sense." Beck shrugged.

"No, he hates hunters, but he reserves a special hate for Rommy," Sam explained as he slowed to a stop by some large rocks.

"Because she took his best friend's son away," Jax added as he finally remembered the hate between his mother and the siren king. It was easy to forget about as most night humans hated his mother. She was notorious for her kills and keeping the night humans away from regular humans.

"We probably want to tell father to contact the siren king," Jax said to Beck. He never pictured Wes as the friend-having type of person.

Beck raised an eyebrow.

"Sam's father is the siren king, and he hates Rommy because she took me away. Since I'm no longer missing …"

"You father is Wesley Cunningham, the First of the vampyre?" Sam now stared at Jax.

Jax shrugged. "Yes, our father is Wes." He had to include Beck. They still didn't seem to believe Beck was his brother.

"Wait. Then that means you two are his heirs," Sam replied.

"Actually, only Jax is his heir. I was killed over a decade ago and activated my vampyre genes. I can't be his heir because I'm not his living son," Beck explained. He was talking more with Sam than he ever did when Jax had a question. Jax was beginning to think it was a night human thing.

Jax didn't want to spend more time on something that he wasn't sure he was fine with talking about.

"So how do we get to the island? I thought your friend made it a magical prison." Jax turned to Whitney.

"She did, but since the only source of our healing water is there, we had to make a secret channel into the auditorium to access it when needed," Whitney explained. "Wait until you see what I made for you since you can't breathe in water."

Jax nodded along with Beck who had a much stiffer nod—like he was forcing himself to agree. Beck was definitely showing signs of hating water, and Jax was trying to think of ways to use that to his advantage the next time they sparred. Jax thought his older brother didn't have a single weakness, but it was possible there was one after all.

"Are you sure we never met?" Whitney turned to Beck. "Have you ever hunted in Florida? Are you a fan of Sam's? Maybe I saw you at a concert?"

Sam was the lead singer in a band. He hid from the hunters for years being a singer which was beyond ironic as the siren were known for being able to control humans with their singing voice. Jax actually had considered joining Sam on tour just to get away from his mother before he decided to find his father. Beck shook his head to answer Whitney.

"How about in Washington, with the witches and skinwalkers?"

"Why would that matter to you?" Beck asked.

"Whitney used to be a skinwalker," Jax replied for her as she continued to study Beck. Beck's eyes shot open in surprise. "Another long story," Jax added. This one he knew.

Whitney grinned at him.

"Wait, so you used to be a skinwalker, and now are an

Oceanid ... whatever that is?" Beck asked for clarification. "Anything else, too?"

Whitney laughed. "Nope, but I'm only eighteen. Maybe I'll find something else to be when I'm in my twenties."

Sam pulled her to himself as he grumbled, "You better not."

"You're serious. She was a different night human before?" Beck asked Jax as Whitney snuggled into Sam's arms.

"Completely serious. Witches took away her skinwalker side and left her human only for her to be turned by Sam."

Beck stared in amazement. Whitney noticed him watching her, so she wiggled out of Sam's arms.

"I still say there's something really familiar about you. And no, Sam, I'm not hitting on him. No one is as cute as you are." Whitney didn't turn to Sam as she rolled her eyes. "So are you two ready to go for a swim?" She dropped it, but Jax could tell she was still studying Beck.

Beck looked around, confused. There was no beach nearby. They were standing in trees. Jax just shrugged. He figured they'd have to swim to the island. But what did it matter when you had mermaids as your guide? He wasn't worried in the least. Pulling off his shirt and kicking off his shoes, he was ready to see if his theory was correct. And if not, what was the worst it would be, a little pain? He could handle that.

Jax had no problem jumping into unknown waters because he trusted his friends. Whitney and Sam weren't about to let him die. Beck seemed to hesitate like he wanted to ask questions, but kept his mouth shut. Where was his I'm a night human—I can do anything spirit?

"We'll go first and make sure it's safe for you," Whitney explained as she moved a few feet closer to what Jax now knew was the edge of a rock cliff.

Sam nodded as he walked up beside her. Without another word, they both jumped and transformed as they fell in the air to the ocean below. Jax smiled as Whitney's pink tail plunged into the water. Pink was the perfect color for her tail, as pink was the best color to describe her personality.

Jax moved closer to the edge and looked below. Whitney and Sam surfaced and motioned for them to jump.

"We're night humans, right?" Jax said to Beck. "We're invincible."

Without hesitation, Jax stepped off the edge of the cliff as Beck added, "But you can still drown, as you're still human."

Beck was quickly beside Jax, falling into the unknown water. Jax didn't let Beck's words affect him, even though he caught the part that only Jax could drown. He really needed to learn more about the vampyre. During their walk was the second time that Beck explained that he had died. Was it really possible to come back from death? Jax understood that the vampyre multiplied by drinking blood and dying, but Jax assumed it was a fake death, like slowed heartbeat to the point that people thought they were dead. He didn't think they actually died. He was going to have to ask his father for more details.

As the water neared, Jax held his breath and plunged under. Jumping feet first, instead of diving like the two mer, made Jax able to kick easily to the surface. Jax came out of the water to where Whitney, Sam, and Beck were waiting. The slow day human was the last to surface, of course.

"So I created this really cool air tunnel close the island that you and Beck can go through so you can breathe," Whitney explained as she popped up directly in front of Jax.

"How far do we have to swim?" Beck asked as he treaded water beside Jax.

"Oh, it's too far for you to swim. It'd take forever. Sam and I'll just take you guys," Whitney replied. Sam surfaced beside Whitney. "Hang on like a piggyback ride," Whitney ordered Jax.

Jax wrapped his arms around Whitney's neck. He could feel the push of her tail as they shot forward in the water. He didn't have time to look back and see if Beck was coming or not as Whitney was correct. There was no way he could swim as fast as her. Jax closed his eyes when the water started to spray in his face. It wasn't like he knew where they were going or could make it back without Whitney, but he wasn't worried. He trusted her completely. She was one of the good night humans.

As fast as they started, Whitney pulled to a sudden stop. Jax began to let go, but she placed a hand on his arms to stop him.

"No. I just wanted to warn you that were are going under now," she explained.

"You know I can't breathe underwater, right?" Jax didn't want to glance into the deep water beneath them.

"I know that, silly. I got all sorts of cool water tricks now that I'm officially an Oceanid. I made this tunnel for your head to go through, so we don't have to worry. I made it for you and your brother, but if he's dead, then he doesn't breathe air, right?"

"I have no clue. I never learned much about vampyre because they were thought to be extinct." Jax shrugged, though she couldn't see him.

"I'm finding extinct doesn't mean the same thing in the night human world. Are you ready?"

"Sure," Jax answered. He was pretty certain Oceanid were extinct, too, but here was Whitney, an Oceanid. He had to make a mental note to look up all the extinct night human clans. He had a feeling he'd be seeing more of them in the future.

Without further warning, Jax felt himself being pulled into the water. Reflexively he held his breath, but soon found he wasn't getting wet. Jax held his breath as long as he could because he could see the water all around him. They were diving deeper under the water before Whitney propelled them forward. With his last energy gone, Jax gasped and was surprised to find there was air. He really wasn't getting wet. With all the anxiety of having to hold his breath gone, Jax looked up into the ocean above him. He could see fish passing by and the light of the sky but guessed he was down at least ten feet or more.

Whitney pulled Jax along, and he kind of wanted to be able to see behind himself to see how Beck was handling their ocean dip. It was beyond weird. He felt the water rushing over his body as Whitney pulled him, but his head was dry. He hadn't ever gone snorkeling or scuba diving since night humans were found on land, but he had a feeling it felt like he did now, without the dry head.

After a bit, Whitney changed their trajectory, and they began to ascend to the surface. Jax wouldn't have minded longer in the water as the experience was a once-in-a-lifetime thing, but he knew they had to be in and out of the island quickly. Whitney had already warned him that the island's inmates didn't like visitors. The battle last year on the island had left the mer who didn't want to behave trapped, but they couldn't move the healing water, so it was also trapped with the human-hating mer.

They surfaced by a stone wall.

"There are climbing spots here," Whitney explained as she began to climb, effortlessly turning back into a human with legs, fully clothed. She was lucky to be one of the few night humans that could transform shape and keep her clothing. For only being a mermaid for just about a year, she was great at it.

Jax followed Whitney as they began climbing the stone wall. He heard Beck and Sam break the surface behind them, but kept his concentration on the hand and foot holds instead of looking back like he wanted to. He really was tempted to glance at his perfect older brother all dripping with water. It might help not to see him as perfect, but then again, water probably ran from Beck.

As they reached the top, Jax found they were exactly where he expected, but this was certainly not how he got there the last time he had been on the siren island. They were standing in the siren amphitheater. Whitney had explained to him the last time he had been on the island that it was a place for meetings and gaining access to the siren healing water. Since the siren no longer lived on the island, it was just a place to access the water. The long rows were eerily silent.

"What's the plan?" Sam asked as he and Beck approached from behind them.

Jax shrugged. Of course, Beck's hair was perfectly styled even though it was wet. Jax had doubts that he was himself really their father's heir. Beck was beyond a much better pick. Beck raised an eyebrow at Jax as he caught him staring.

"I need to remove this tattoo," Jax told Sam as he pointed to the large Celtic cross on his arm. "I've tried to do it myself but if I cut shallow, it heals too much, and if I cut too deep, I lose too much blood."

Sam nodded like it made perfect sense to skin yourself to remove a tattoo. Beck was gritting his teeth already. Jax figured Beck had to have some clue what he was doing, but it seemed his brother hadn't thought he was serious when he said he was going to remove it.

"I was hoping the healing water would make me able to remove it without dying from blood loss," Jax continued.

Whitney seemed to be considering it. She was as cautious as Beck when it came to Jax's life.

"We skinned your scales off last year, and yet you

healed perfectly," Jax added fact to his argument. It was true. When Whitney needed him to, Jax and his sister, Jade, helped her skin her mermaid tail to get the scales to save the mer that were good. It was the healing water that saved her, and he was positive it would save him, too.

"Does the water work on non-night humans?" Whitney asked Sam. Jax hadn't thought of that.

"He's not a day human," Beck replied. "He's a night human, but he just can't access that side yet." Beck sounded like he was supporting the idea.

"The water can heal anyone," Sam replied.

"And I can direct the water right to you," Whitney added as she waved a hand and the small drizzle of water falling down the stone wall beside them was diverted to where they stood.

"Good. Who's going to help me cut this off?" Jax asked.

Beck stepped back. "I can't."

Jax looked surprised at his brother. He didn't seem to have a problem pulverizing him each time they fought in practice.

"I can't cut you because you are the lord of the clan," Beck explained.

"Um, no. That's our father," Jax replied. He had really hoped he would help. Jax wasn't too keen on cutting himself again. He had almost passed out the last time he tried.

"And as the heir, it's also you," Beck answered as he turned back to the small opening where the ocean was.

Jax sighed. Well, he wasn't getting any help there.

Sam leaned in quick and took the knife from Jax's belt.

"I got your back," Sam told him, twirling the knife in his hand. "And really, Whitney has our back so we can't screw up."

"And don't worry, Beck, if this was going to kill me, wouldn't this be one of those times my future flashes would help?" Jax had fun being able to use that back at his brother. Beck shook his head but didn't turn around.

Whitney flashed a smile at Sam and Jax. If it had been five years earlier, Jax would have never imagined doing what he was going to do, but he didn't fear it at all now. He trusted Sam, and more than that he trusted Whitney. There was nothing but good in that mer.

Jax took a deep breath and laid his forearm on the stone slab that was in the middle of the stage. He wrapped the chain that was used to tie down the mer during ceremonies to hold onto his wrist before clenching it in his hand.

With one last look at Beck, who was still staring at the ocean, Jax turned to his two friends. "Let's do this."

Coming home had been hard. Sam had cut off the tattoo as Jax had asked, and it had changed nothing. It wasn't the answer Jax had been hoping for. To say Jax was disappointed was an understatement. He was devastated. Simone was getting sicker, and Jax couldn't help her. He did his best to thank his friends and promised to visit again as soon as he could.

Jax sat on his bed with his head in his hands. He had

tried in vain the whole way home to transform on his own, but it didn't work. He had felt a change the moment the tattoo was removed, but it wasn't a change to let him be a night human. He was still stuck in his day human form and was nowhere closer to finding a cure for Simone.

He moved to the middle of his bedroom floor and sat down with his legs crossed. They had one class in meditation during their hunter training, but it didn't take well for most of the people. Hunters weren't the calm, think happy thoughts type of people. They were more the act first and think on the go type. Jax found it useless then, but he was hoping there was something in it now that would help him.

Taking a deep breath, Jax closed his eyes. He counted to ten like he had been taught and took a second deep breath. He tried his best to calm himself and attempted to look inward. Beck had explained that his night human side was always there inside of him, even when he was a day human, and that Jax had a hidden night human side also. Jax just needed to find that part and connect with it. Taking another deep breath, he searched his mind for something dark and blood lusting. He found nothing. The monster he knew that was inside of him was still locked down.

Kicking his legs out, Jax smashed into his desk chair and broke the leg. He looked up and felt bad at his hunter strength. He needed somewhere safer to get his anger out.

Quickly, Jax threw on a pair of gym shorts and headed to the basement. The basement was the workout room that he spent many hours in getting beat up by Beck. It didn't hold the best memories, but everything there was night human safe, and he could pound away at it. Jax didn't hesitate to go over to the hanging bags and begin to throw punches.

It wasn't fair. He didn't ask to be born a mysterious hunter. He didn't want to be one. They didn't want him, and he didn't want them. Why couldn't he break free? Jax hit the bag harder now as his anger grew.

Why couldn't he save Simone? Here he was being named heir to a whole clan of night humans, and it did no good. He still couldn't save her. She was dying. And there was nothing more he could think of to do. Jax swung again, increasing his power, and he felt the rafter above him where the bag was chained to shift.

Jax didn't want to be a night human, and he sure didn't want to be a hunter. He didn't want to be either. He wanted to go live his life without knowledge of any of the things that go bump in the night. He wanted to be free of all of it. What had the night human world ever done for him?

Jax didn't think as he swung again at the bag. He heard a snap and stepped back as the bag went flying across the room. Jax stood in shock, staring at the bag that left a dent in the cement wall. There was no way possible he had done that. Beck had explained that the gym was set up to hold against his strength. There was no way Jax was stronger than Beck. Jax looked up at the creaking rafter. He didn't need to stick around and see if the crack was bad. Jax needed to get out of the house and clear his head.

Taking the stairs two at a time, Jax flew up them and outside before anyone could come searching for him. He wasn't one for losing his temper, and he could see it was a good idea to keep it in check. His night human side might have still been sealed away, but it didn't mean he couldn't access that power; he just couldn't do it intentionally.

Jax began a jog around the property. When he first moved in with his father, he had mapped out a route that would be exactly ten miles. It was a good morning jog for him, and sometimes an afternoon jog also. Jax began his run and was happy to be breathing in clean air and to have the opportunity to clear his head. He was also happy it was daytime, and thus it was likely that there was only Beck around to run into. As he picked up his pace to his normal run, Jax could feel the air getting thicker. He slowed a bit. It was like how he felt magic.

Cautiously walking back the way he came, Jax kept his eyes peeled for trouble as he sucked in his breath. Magic now, too? What more was life going to throw his way? Jax smacked his hand on the railing as he began to climb back up the stairs to the porch of his father's house. Now he couldn't even take a nice run without trouble. His life was getting worse by the minute. Jax pulled back his hand and rubbed it. His palm was red and sore. Confused, he walked across the porch to the swing and sat down. He didn't hit the railing that hard, and his hunter healing should have kicked in to take away the pain.

"Bad day?" Jen asked, and Jax finally noticed she was sitting in a rocking chair down the porch from him.

"You could call it that," Jax replied as he continued to look around the yard. He was still worried about the magic he felt. He knew his father didn't fear the witches, but the New Orleans clan was a powerful coven.

"So it didn't work?" Jen asked as she sipped her coffee. She had been more reserved since she had moved in at the same time as Jax. Breaking her bracelet and letting out her night human had done something to her, or maybe finding her father had.

"No. And I'm out of ideas. I have to sit here and watch her die because I can't figure it out," Jax stated, defeated. "And the worst part is I feel like I'm falling apart. I broke the punching bag downstairs only to have hitting the railing hurt my hand. I'm not keeping my hunter side in check, and it's only going to get worse as Simone gets worse. We're taught as hunter children to channel our energy into fighting, but there's no fight left in me. Just anger."

Jen nodded. She looked very much like Jade, and it made Jax miss her. He wasn't certain he would be allowed to speak with her if he called and he didn't want to call until he saved Simone. Only that didn't look like it was going to happen, and Jax dreaded what the call would be like once she did die.

"It sounds like how I felt when I removed my bracelet," Jen added as she watched Jax more closely.

"Exactly what I was thinking," Wes added as he walked up the stairs. Jax had no idea where his father materialized from. "I've talked with my contacts, and a small, magic-infused tattoo is put on hunter children right after they are born, but again, they're born human.

It sounds like the tattoo was just a means for channeling the night human energy."

Moaning, Jax put his head in his hands. It made much more sense. He felt the magic rip from him when he removed the tattoo. It had to be the same magic as Jen's bracelet. He didn't open his night human side, but he had weakened his control over it. He didn't think things could get worse, but they had. He needed to find a way to unlock his night human side if he ever wanted control again.

CHAPTER 6

"**I just don't** think the witches would help the hunters," Beck argued. Jax sat in his father's office, listening while his older brother and father talked. He wasn't about to jump in. Right now he had very little control of his emotions and was afraid he would either explode or cry, neither of which would get him very far with either man in the room. Jax couldn't imagine his father had ever cried; the man barely smiled.

"The witches around here hate us," Wes replied. "I could easily see them offering services to the hunters."

Jax wasn't sure if the witches hated night humans or just Wes who had cost them their latest coven leader when she gave her life to bind Jen's night human side inside of her with a magical bracelet. Jax was pretty sure they hated him specifically. He had met a witch once, and she didn't seem to hate anyone. In her area, the witches married night humans. He doubted they were the same ones, but again, he couldn't voice his opinion.

"The witches are fickle. They hate us one year and love us the next. I don't think any clan has ever held a clear stance on us. I think we have to look at night humans with magic," Beck countered. "We need someone that has always hated us, someone that has always been on their side, and don't say humans. They couldn't do this. Heck, most of them don't even know about us."

Wes tapped his fingers on his mahogany desk as he stood there in thought. Beck must have made a good argument. Whatever the case, Jax was hoping it meant he could go somewhere soon to do something about his fluctuating night human powers. He didn't dare see Simone with his powers unstable. He could hurt her without meaning to. Jax grasped the edge of the white-and-navy striped chair he was sitting on. He felt his nails poke through the fabric as his anger rose.

"Magical night humans." Wes paused as he tapped more. The tapping was driving Jax nuts, but so was the lack of answers. "I can think of three clans in particular that had magic in them, but I don't think night humans would help the hunters. It would have to be a reclusive group that didn't care about either night humans or the hunters."

Wes tapped as he thought. Jax, meanwhile, was getting fed up. They needed to stop sitting and thinking and start doing. He felt his anger getting close to popping, and he wouldn't be able to contain it if it did.

"I was thinking more along the lines of visiting Devin," Beck replied. The anger inside of Jax stopped at the mention of the older brother he had yet to meet.

Wes nodded. "But are you ready to do that yet?"

Beck shrugged, pushing his hands through his perfectly styled blond hair.

"I'm not sure fifteen years is enough time," Wes added cautiously.

"I'm not sure there's ever the right amount of time.

He's going to be mad whether I go now or in a couple years."

"Make sure you prep Jax before you leave," Wes instructed and waved his hand, dismissing them.

Jax followed Beck out the door and into the hallway. Beck didn't stop and walked right out the front door of the house. Jax was unsure what to say. It wasn't like Beck was open with details, but he had no clue what was going on. Devin was Beck's younger brother, but he wasn't sure why the guy would be mad at Beck.

"Do you have enough of Father's blood to make it through a weekend?" Beck asked as he walked over to his parked car.

"Another trip?" Jax asked. They were running out of time. Driving all over the place hadn't yielded results yet.

"Get your stuff now. I'm leaving in two minutes with or without you." That was at least kind of an answer to the question. Trip it was.

Jax fled upstairs and grabbed his bag, again without knowing any details. He tried his best as the anger was starting to build again, and he had no way to control it. Taking a deep breath, Jax attempted to steady the flow that was like a volcano getting ready to erupt. He threw in the vial of blood sitting on the shelf by his bed as Beck had ordered. He didn't want to be a night human, and he didn't want to be using his father's blood. He wanted to save Simone. Why didn't anyone else care about that?

Why was Beck allowed to order him around? Jax was the heir, not Beck. Jax could feel his irrational anger take over. There was nothing he could do to stop it. Without thinking, Jax swung out and hit the wall next to his bed. His fist went right through. Jax pulled back his clean hand, not a scratch, and let out a breath. He felt better, but the wall didn't. When Jen got back, she was going to be upset seeing as how they now shared the space. Jax didn't have time to fix it as he bolted out the door at the sound of Beck's car starting up.

The trip to see his older brother, Devin, was actually a lot more complicated than going to meet up with JoAnne, and yet Beck still didn't use a map. It was like he knew exactly where to go, and Jax wanted to know if that was a Beck thing or a night human vampyre thing. When he finally got control of his night human side, would Jax be able to go anywhere without looking at a map? He hadn't heard of that being a night human trait, but he was looking forward to it. Hunters, in general, had a sense of north, east, south, and west, but not what road led where.

Beck continued to drive silently as they made their way into the Appalachian Mountains. Jax didn't ask any questions even though he wanted to know what was going on. He had decided, after putting a Jax-fist-sized hole in the wall back in his room, he needed to focus on his meditation and breathing exercises for the trip so that he didn't do anything that would make it take longer. Simone was failing, and they needed answers quickly; not spending time on dealing with his anger issues.

Jax kept his eyes closed as he took deep breaths. He was worried they wouldn't find an answer in time to save

Simone, and he was slightly concerned that he was going to stay in this in-between state of constant fluctuation of power. He had never been taught what to do if the night human powers that made him a hunter failed. In fact, as a hunter, there was no option to fail. You either succeeded, or you died. That was it.

"Our brother is part of the sidhe," Beck said as the car continued to wind up the mountainside.

Jax opened his eyes to look at Beck and see if he was serious. The sidhe stayed out of all night human and day human politics. In fact, Jax was pretty sure the sidhe had nothing to do with anyone but themselves. Little was known about them, and there was no hunter interaction with them on the books. How was it possible that his day human brother was with them?

"Don't they have some sort of rule that keeps day humans out?" Jax asked, referencing a story he had once heard about them.

"Good thing we aren't day humans," Beck replied with a strained smile.

Jax didn't need to be a genius to see that this was hard on Beck. He wasn't sure what to say to his older brother. He wasn't sure what he'd do himself if he hadn't seen his sister in a long time.

"Is Devin still human?" Jax was pretty sure he was, but it was the way Beck said it that made him wonder. Jax knew very little about his other older brother. As usual, Beck was tight-lipped on that subject.

"Yes," Beck replied.

"So he's stuck there?" That would make perfect sense as to why Devin would be mad at Beck. Beck was this awesome night human hunter, and he hadn't even rescued his little brother. For as much as Beck followed Jax around keeping him safe, that seemed out of character, but it made it seem so much more clear.

"No. He's not stuck. He rules them."

Okay, that made no sense at all.

"Why don't you want to do this?" Jax asked what had been on his mind for hours. Beck seemed to be in the sharing mood, and Jax hoped it would continue.

"I haven't seen Devin since I was killed. He doesn't know I'm alive," Beck stated as he continued to look only at the road.

"Wait." Sitting up, Jax stared at Beck. "You've let your little brother think you've been dead all these years? How long has it been? Really? Dead?" Jax was shocked. He wasn't allowed to speak with Jade openly since he wasn't a hunter anymore, but if something happened and she thought he was dead, and he wasn't, he wouldn't let her mourn him. He would let her know some way that he was still alive, even if they couldn't talk. That was all sorts of messed up.

Beck shrugged. "Technically, I'm still dead. All vampyre are dead. The only reason I can turn back into a day human is from being our father's son. If I was a normal vampyre, I would be a night human all the time just like everyone else. I didn't think there was a need to tell Devin I was still walking around if it was still dead. I wasn't ever going to be the brother he had once."

Jax just shook his head. How could Beck be so heartless? Devin had to have been mourning him. Without knowing about their father, Devin had to think he was all alone in the world. Beck let his little brother be alone. What sort of older brother was he?

"We were killed by a night human. When I turned into one, I didn't want to see Devin again because I didn't want him to know I was a monster just like the one that killed our parents. I knew nothing of this world, and neither did he. Even though our mother was a hunter, she never told us about night humans. That one night was like a nightmare. It was easier to let him think I was dead."

"Easier for you or him?"

Beck didn't reply, letting Jax know he hit the nail on the head with that comment.

"So we can expect that this isn't going to be a fun family reunion?" Jax had to be the one to start the conversation again. He needed to know what he was walking into. His hunter side always had to be prepared.

"It was never meant to be," Beck replied as he swerved around another turn. The roads had gotten curvier as they drove higher into the mountains. "We're here to see if Devin knows how the night human side is sealed. That's it. I don't need to know anything else. He doesn't need to know anything more either. I've kept tabs on him. He's safe and happy. He has a mate and is still a day human. He'll never be the monster I am. I've never wanted him to think he has to join our father and me. I want him to stay here and live his life. We go in and get our answers, and we go home. That's our mission."

Laying back, Jax closed his eyes. Cold, Beck was so cold. He needed to calm down. Why was Beck being so callous? Then again, what did Jax expect? Beck was a night human. They were all like that. Something about becoming a monster included losing your humanity for most of them. That was one of the million reasons Jax didn't want to be one. Not that he had a choice now. He doubted that he could return to the hunters and ask for the magical tattoo back to regulate his powers. He was going to be one no matter what he wanted. Not willingly, but he was going to turn into a heartless monster. Maybe he would let Jade think he was dead, too.

The night human world was always around Jax. He never knew what it was like to not know about it, but he had to wonder what it had been like for Beck growing up. Maybe that was part of becoming a night human. If his reality had been crushed with the knowledge of what was really out there, would he become different, too? Jax had met hundreds of night humans. Not all of them were bad. Whitney and Sam were proof that good ones existed, but Jax had seen that there were more bad ones than good ones. He could never tell his father the truth. Jax didn't want to be one of the bad ones, and he wasn't sure how you didn't go that way.

Beck stopped the car, and the engine died. Jax opened his eyes and looked around. He had expected a house or something. They were in a parking lot that was in the middle of nowhere. It was literally trees as far as Jax could see. So far he had no clue how they were going to visit Devin. Then again, why would he know since Beck liked to keep details to himself almost all the time? Beck stepped out of the car, and Jax followed down the sidewalk. A parking lot with maybe thirty spaces and a sidewalk. More than a little strange. It was a sidewalk in the woods. Jax had an idea what they were doing now. He had no choice but to follow Beck as he walked down the random sidewalk. Jax glanced at the large board, the only thing not of nature, marking out trails as they walked by.

"Hiking?" Jax asked. From the sign, he found they were in the middle of a national park, and Beck was walking toward the hiking trails. Still didn't make a whole lot of sense. He had never heard of people going missing from the trails and one thing all night human had in common was needing human blood. Hiding in the woods didn't work really well when it came to that. "We go hiking to find them?" It really wasn't the time to be hiking, but Jax wasn't the one leading the way.

"They will find us. This is all sidhe territory, and as soon as they sense us, someone will come. Night humans can sense when people come into their territory. We don't share well."

Didn't share well? Marching into other clans' territories and upsetting them didn't sound like a fun plan to Jax. He could barely keep his temper in check as it was. What if someone challenged him? What would he do? Beck kept walking without explaining more, like usual. At least Jax was able to keep that from bothering him … for now. Maybe the fresh air in the mountains would do him some good.

Beck led the way into the forest and onto the trail.

"Alum falls here we come," Jax muttered to himself, knowing Beck could hear him but didn't care.

The scenery was nice as they hiked and the fresh air was actually good, too. Jax took in the beauty of the greenery around him as they moved farther into the forest and forgot about his problems. He didn't know how long they had been walking when he felt someone else there. Beck must have sensed it also as he was way better at all the night human stuff, but he didn't flinch. Jax tried to look around casually. He hated being watched, and since he wasn't sure if the eyes were friendly or not, it was a big problem to his fluctuating temper.

"We will rest right up there," Beck told Jax, glancing back at him. "You probably need to take a drink. Father would advise it."

Jax got the hint as they stopped at a bench, but he still hated his brother being bossy. He pulled out a vial of his father's blood and put it in his mouth as Beck handed him a bottle of water to wash it down. Of course, Beck had a bottle of water. Jax finally noticed that Beck was dressed as a hiker with a backpack and a canteen of water. When the heck did he have time to pack or change into that? Jax had to be losing it. It took so much effort to contain his emotions he was missing small details, or maybe big ones. He still wasn't sure yet what all he did miss.

"Tell your leader we need to talk with him," Beck said as he looked into the forest in front of them. From where they sat on the bench, all Jax could see was trees. He felt the night human presence but saw no one. It seemed like Beck was talking to the trees in front of him, not humans.

Within a moment, the night human presence simply

disappeared.

"Um ..." Jax wasn't sure what to say.

"We only have a few minutes before he arrives. No matter what goes on, you keep your mouth shut. Father has a lot of rules and secrecy is the top one. No one must know that the vampyre are alive, and no one can be told you are the heir. We haven't remained hidden this long without rules. Even as the heir, if you break either of those two rules, you'll be cast out."

Jax's eye bugged at his brother's words. It wasn't like he was going around saying that the vampyre were alive, but there wasn't any talk of rules before. Beck had spent hours and hours training Jax in the arts of defending himself, yet he failed to mention either of these rules or anything else that would get him kicked out of the clan. He didn't even know he could get kicked out. This was all new to him. Why didn't they tell him everything up front? The vampyre drove him nuts, and the one with him did the best job of all.

It wasn't minutes they had to wait as someone seemed to step from the trees. The guy just melted out of the tree. Jax wasn't as surprised as Beck. He had seen Whitney's witch friend do that before. What was surprising was the man who stood before them. He had Beck's golden hair and blue eyes. In fact, they could almost pass as twins beyond the fact that the one that came from the trees was glowing. His skin had an actual sheen to it, like he would make a good glow stick.

"Dispel," the glowing man said with authority. How could this be their brother, Beck's little brother at that? Beck had told him he was a day human. He didn't say he was a witch. And he wasn't little.

Jax felt the rush of magic go over his skin. If he hadn't just taken his father's blood, he was pretty sure that his night human side would be raging. With it turned on completely, he felt like he was back in control for the moment. He hated to admit that Beck was right. At least he wasn't going to blow everything with his wild mood swings.

"Well it's good to see you, Ben," the glowing man said quietly.

Beck stood there staring at the man. Neither of them moved. Jax could tell who the tree man was, but Beck had said it had been fifteen years. He was pretty sure Devin was a small kid the last time he saw him. Did he not recognize his own brother? It had to be like looking in a mirror.

"I go by Beck now," Beck explained as he finally found his voice.

Glowing Devin smiled at him. "Of course you need a superhero name now that you're a superhero. I still go by Devin." He smiled, and his teeth glowed brighter than his skin. It made no sense. Devin was glowing and seemed more night human than Beck, but Beck said he wasn't one. Maybe this was a change. Perhaps that was why Beck seemed to be so stuck, staring at him. Maybe Beck didn't know. Or was it Ben? He'd have to ask later about that one.

Feeling out of place, Jax allowed his gaze to bounce between them. Of everything that Beck expected, Jax was sure he didn't expect Devin to be okay seeing him for the first time in fifteen years. Beck had let Devin think all of his family was dead when they weren't. That was something most people would be angry about. Jax hadn't expected him to be fine either, but Devin was. He was smiling; not throwing punches or yelling. He didn't seem to be a bit out of place or upset by seeing Beck.

"So what brings you to this part of the country?" Devin asked as he glanced behind Beck at Jax.

Jax wasn't sure, but he felt like Devin could see everything about him. It was strange, like there were no secrets. It wasn't as if Jax hadn't met tons of night humans before, and in his vampyre form there had been all sorts he'd met just days ago, but it was different with Devin. Perhaps it was the look in his eyes, or maybe there was just something within him, but it felt different. He could definitely feel the night human magic pouring from his older brother, but he was certain that, like Beck, Devin was a day human. But then it was the all-knowing eyes. Day humans didn't see into people like that. Jax stared at him more. It was as if Devin was surrounded by magic, night human magic, but at the same time, he was a day human at his core. It was peculiar, and Jax had no clue what it meant.

"We've run into a little problem and thought maybe you could help," Beck replied, glancing around at the trees.

Jax could feel it then. Devin wasn't alone. There were more night humans around, even if they couldn't see them. Maybe they were doing the magic. Wes had said they needed a clan that did magic. Jax knew very little about the sidhe, but it would make sense that they could.

Beck held out his hand for Devin. Several people

emerged from the shadows. Dressed all in green and brown, they blended right into the woods. Not only did they hide well in shadows, but they were dressed to hide in their environment. Jax was racking his brain for all he knew on the sidhe, which was very little. Mostly it was tales told by the night humans they had encountered, and you couldn't trust a night human, so he thought they were just that—stories. It turned out the whole one with nature thing seemed to be true, and he wondered how much more was as well.

"My lord," one of the forest men said as Devin walked forward to take Beck's hand, "he's an outsider and can't be trusted."

Devin shrugged and grasped Beck's hand anyway. "He's my brother."

The forest men began to chatter, but one look from Devin silenced the whole group. Authority rang from him, stronger than even Beck was when he bossed people around, maybe even stronger than their father. Devin turned back to Beck, and they shared a look that left Jax wondering what it meant.

Releasing his hand, Devin took a step backward. "Welcome to my home, brothers," he said before turning around and walking into the woods.

Beck followed Devin off the trail, and Jax had no choice but to go wandering into the woods with them. Not the best choice, but one he couldn't avoid.

Jax was lost before they had walked more than fifteen minutes. He was more the city type than outdoorsy, but it was too late to say that to Beck. There was nothing Jax could do as Devin silently walked without explanation to where they were going, but to followed him all the same. Jax could feel the people around them watching, and it made him uneasy. Beck—if he felt them, too—didn't seem worried. Jax had to wonder what was shared with their handshake, but as always Beck was tight-lipped, and he seemed to have that in common with Devin.

The woods around him were looked the same as when they started. There were trees and bushes, little flowers here and there, a river trickling somewhere nearby, and even animals scurrying around. Devin wasn't leading them somewhere that looked like a night human hang out. In fact, Jax could still see the sun in the sky—it hadn't yet set. The sidhe must not have to avoid the sun like many of the other night humans did. Jax wished he had more information on them. At this point, he just wished he knew what Beck did. He wasn't completely sure how much older his brother was, but even though he had only been a night human for fifteen years, Jax would like to have his fifteen years of night human knowledge.

Devin paused as they walked into an open grassy area. Jax caught up with his brothers and waited beside them.

"Lindsey, I'm bringing these two night humans into town as my guests," Devin said to the empty space like he was looking at something in the grassy knoll in front of them. If Jax didn't know he lived with night humans, and night humans could be weird, he would have thought this older brother was as crazy as his other older brother.

Devin walked into the grassy knoll and continued

forward. Jax jumped as the hill opened an eye to watch them. He had thought the sidhe following them were hidden well, but he was now pretty sure the hill was the best disguise. Jax couldn't tell where the rest of the creature was; he could only view part of a face from the eyes looking at him. If there were arms and legs, there was no way Jax could avoid being hit because he wouldn't even see them coming. The hill smiled at him.

As Devin stepped onto a bridge, only then did Jax understand where they were actually going. The bridge was made up of the same bushes and trees they had already passed on their hike. Even more so, it looked like everything around them was the same. Jax hadn't noticed the small opening that led over a small river below until Devin stepped onto it. Everything blended so seamlessly. Jax hesitated as he peered down at the water. The branches wove together enough for Devin and Beck to walk with ease, but it still seemed strange to Jax.

"It can be a bit surreal," Devin stated from the other side of the bridge. "But I got used to it, and you will, too. I think they made it to purposely mess with day human senses."

Jax lifted his gaze to see that Devin was talking to him.

"Night humans have no sense of the weird around them, but as a day human, I promise you, I know what weird is. I've been here a couple years and still find it can be strange at times," Devin added.

But Devin wasn't a day human, and Jax could see that. He smelled like magic and glowed. Day humans didn't glow.

"But you still think it's beautiful," a girl with dark, curly hair said as she walked up and looped her arms around Devin's. With her free hand, she offered it to Beck. "Hi. I'm Devin's wife, Nessa," she said. Taking her hand, Beck shook it. "So glad you both could come to visit him. Devin won't even invite Arianna to visit, and she's like a sister to us."

Visit? Jax was pretty sure it wasn't a visiting occasion, but he wasn't going to tell the girl wearing a crown that. From the looks of the few people around them, and the people who bowed as she walked past, he was pretty sure there was something more to that crown than just holding back her curls. Devin being part of the sidhe was making a lot more sense now.

Devin and his wife led the way down the street they were now on. People around them moved out of the way without a word as Devin neared, and most bowed down to them as soon as they were seen. No one seemed to pay attention to Jax and Beck beyond the same men from before, who were following. They continued scowling at them as they held tightly to their weapons. Jax had a feeling the sidhe still felt that Beck and he were a threat.

Jax took a walk—during which time Devin's wife talked to Beck and asked a ton of questions—as a means to look around. There was nothing known about the reclusive sidhe, and Jax could see why. Even if someone stumbled upon them, unless the people were outside and you saw them open a door, you wouldn't see the homes. They blended seamlessly into the nature around them. Some homes seemed to be large trees, and other bushes or even hills. It was like nature conformed to what was needed, and the people let it be. Everything was green and alive, much different than the life Jax had lived going from city to city his whole life.

When they reached one of the first obvious structures, a fence made of trees packed so tightly you couldn't pass, Jax had the feeling they were at their destination. The people following them stopped outside the tree wall as Devin led the way through. One last guy gave a look to Devin before a deep bow.

On the other side of the trees was an open grassy courtyard. A squeal sounded as a small child, who couldn't be much older than a year, began to toddle over to them. Devin reached down and picked up the child who giggled with joy.

"Your niece," Devin said to Beck as he handed off the child to his wife.

"Daddy can play later," Devin's wife told the child as she looked up to Devin. He kissed the child's forehead and then his wife's before they left in one direction, and Devin led Beck and Jax in the other way.

"So what's the business that brought you out here?" Devin asked as they walked into an open courtyard on the side of the building that his wife and child just went into.

"Is it safe to talk?" Beck asked as he looked around.

Jax focused his senses and took a deep breath. Even though he couldn't feel the night humans that continued protecting Devin, he could smell them. They were still there, though they didn't come within the wall of trees.

"It's quiet inside the room there." Devin motioned to a doorway that seemed to spring open on its own. Jax wouldn't have seen it otherwise.

Jax followed his two brothers as they went inside. He would have pinched himself if he thought he wasn't being watched. The sidhe were called faeries, and he completely agreed. He could see leaves growing on the side of the building, and if he looked down, the plants that made up walls were still rooted in the ground. The building really was growing.

To his surprise, the inside of the structure actually looked like a normal building. There was an empty front entryway, and the stone floor pathway led down a hallway filled with doors. Devin turned and went into the first room, and Beck followed. Jax stepped into the room that looked like a meeting room of sorts with tables and chairs set in a circle. There was someone in the back corner of a table with her back to them. She had the same dark, almost black hair as Devin's wife.

"Cassie, can you set up a mute spell?" Devin asked.

The girl turned around, and Jax had to stop himself from staring. He knew who she was. It was Whitney's best friend—the witch. What was she doing in the sidhe village?

Cassie walked over to the doorway and closed it. With a brush of her hand, magic pulsated around them. Jax caught his breath as it felt like the air was knocked from him. Beck didn't move, as to be expected from Jax's perfect older brother. And it seemed Devin was just as perfect. Neither of them acted as anything happened. They had to have felt the magic, too. Show-offs, Jax decided as they continued to just stare at each other like they were having a silent conversation.

Devin took a seat in one of the chairs that was sitting in the circle in the middle of the room. Pulling out another chair, Beck sat down also. Jax wasn't sure if he was invited or not, so he stood awkwardly by the door. Cassie went back to her table and disregarded everything and everybody.

"We've run into a little problem that we think is magically related," Beck started out.

"Then why not see the witches?" Cassie asked from her spot in the corner of the room. So she wasn't really ignoring them after all.

Smiling, Devin turned back to Beck. "Yes, as she said. Why not seek out the witches?"

"Because we're pretty certain the witches aren't involved. We are looking for magic that's used on hunters. Something they use to help them. We assume the witches wouldn't all agree to help hunters, so they couldn't be the source."

Cassie looked at Beck and nodded. "That's true. While some covens do like the hunters, none would openly help them. They'd be afraid of the backlash from the other covens. My coven especially would fight anything helping the hunters since our mates are all night humans." Cassie turned back to her work on the table.

"And the magic we're looking for is night human-related, so we wondered if the sidhe were involved," Beck added.

"We?" Devin asked. Jax was wondering what went on between Jax and Beck in the woods, but it didn't seem to be a family history lesson. He had no clue how Devin knew he was his brother.

"Jax, I, and our biological father," Beck replied and waited.

Jax held his breath, wondering what Devin would think of that.

Devin shrugged. "So that's who've you been with all these years?"

Beck shrugged back. They were like a mirror, so much alike. "On and off. Mostly I stick with the night hunters, but sometimes get called on by our father." Beck nodded his head to Jax at the mention of "our". That seemed to be enough for Devin. He didn't ask further about Beck's past.

"What sort of magic are you looking to break?" Devin got back to the task at hand. Focused on the mission seemed to be a family trait in Devin, too.

"The hunter seal," Beck answered not beating around the bush.

Smiling, Devin nodded, like he had been expecting that. "They wouldn't like that much." Devin seemed to know about it without needing much of an explanation.

Beck laughed a little, and Jax turned to his older brother, shocked. Yes, he'd seen him smile on occasion, but never outright laugh at a joke.

"We don't want to run around turning them into night humans," Beck added with a smile. "Though that would be fun. We want to break the seal on a couple specific people. That's all."

"Like Jax?"

Jax stayed in his spot by the door. He hadn't told Devin his name, and with his father's blood in him, he should have seemed like a night human completely.

Maybe the blood didn't work. Perhaps he was losing control of his night human side. Jax felt the sharp teeth in his mouth. He was still a night human. That was twice now that Devin mentioned Jax being a day human. How did Devin know otherwise?

"Jax and another one need the seal off of them. There's a girl who is dying that we need to help."

Devin nodded as Beck spoke. He turned his eyes to Jax, who was still confused by this all-knowing brother.

"I know what you are because I used to use blood like that all the time. I can smell your blood and your father's mixing. A night human only smells like one person," Devin explained in response to Jax's obvious confusion. Jax lifted up a hand and took a whiff. He didn't smell a difference. Yep, older brother number two was also perfect. Great. They must have taken all the perfect genes, and Jax was left being the one that couldn't keep up. He was never going to live up to two perfect older brothers. Life couldn't get much harder.

"So why do you think it's magic sealing in their night human side?" Devin asked, turning back to Beck.

"A lot of reasons. This would be easier," Beck stated as he pulled out a knife and sliced his hand. Tossing the knife to Devin, Beck held his hand out. Devin did the same.

Jax watched as they clasped bloody cut hands and closed their eyes. The room grew quiet, and the two brothers sat in silence, sharing thoughts and memories through their blood connection.

"You can have a seat," Cassie said from across the room. "This might take a while."

Jax walked over to where she was. There were bottles and ingredients spread all over the table. She pushed back the vials near one of the seats, indicating that he should sit there.

"You're Whitney's friend, right?"

Cassie grinned. "I thought you looked familiar, but I wasn't sure."

Jax smiled, and his tongue touched his sharp night human fangs. He immediately closed his mouth. He didn't need to scare her.

"It's the night human thing. Makes you look just different enough that people don't recognize you," Jax added.

"My night human side only makes me glow in the dark," Cassie replied, putting a paper over her arm and showing her very slight glow. Jax looked surprised. He hadn't noticed before. Cassie did have a slight glow, but not like Devin.

"I wouldn't have known."

Cassie smiled. "I'm a half-breed, so it isn't as strong as everyone else."

Jax finally noticed a jet black cat sitting against the wall as it rumbled a small growl. Jax froze where he sat. It wasn't a cat. Way too large for that. It was a panther. A full-size panther.

Cassie rolled her eyes at the cat, and it laid its head back down on its paws.

"Jared doesn't like the term half-breed."

"Jared?" Jax asked. "You named a panther?"

Cassie grinned. "No. His mom named him."

Jax shook his head. Now that made very little sense,

but he was in a fairy hut with two not completely human brothers who hadn't seen each other in fifteen years, and he had only just recently met himself. Life was keeping up strangely.

"So you're a hunter, right?" Cassie kept mixing as she talked. Jax nodded at her question. "Then why are you all fanged out?"

Jax glanced back at Beck. He was still frozen in place with Devin, and he wasn't sure what he was allowed to say.

"They'll be like that for a while, trading memories. Devin likes to be thorough," she explained as she continued to look Jax over.

"I used to be a hunter," Jax replied in answer to her question.

He figured he had to keep the vampyre a secret, but anything on the hunters was fair game since he wasn't one now. "But I don't want to be one. I found out in the past couple of weeks that hunters have kids with night humans, so us children of the two should be night humans, but something keeps us from being one. The hunters use some kind of magic to keep us day humans when we should have been born night humans. I just want to be a night human now."

"Aww, I get that. You want control over choosing what to be."

Jax hadn't thought of it that way, but it was true. He wanted to choose what he was going to be. So far everyone else was choosing for him.

"Why did you guys come here? The sidhe have nothing to do with the hunters," Cassie added, reaching for a vial with black-colored powder in it. "The only hunters I've ever met were the ones on the siren island that came with you."

"We think the hunters use magic to lock away the night human side of us. I want to be able to unlock it. I thought it was in my tattoo, but cutting it off didn't change anything." Jax didn't know why he was explaining it all to the girl they hadn't come to visit, but he felt like there was something about her he trusted. As a half-breed, as she called herself, he had a feeling she understood being caught between two worlds.

Cassie reached out and touched the very spot where the tattoo had been. She closed her eyes as she whispered some words and then nodded. Slowly her grip became harder and harder. Jax felt the skin start to burn, and he tried to pull back his arm. Her grip was too tight for him to do anything. She was strong for being such a small thing. The burning instantly faded as she opened her eyes.

"I can't change the seal keeping you human. It isn't any magic I've ever seen. Not witch or sidhe, but rather something completely different. But I did put the tattoo magic back. That was witch magic," Cassie replied as she looked back at the stuff in front of her. "And now I need more rosemary."

Jax stared at his arm. There were the four fingerprints burned into his skin where she had grabbed him.

"I agree," Devin said from his seat in the middle of the room. "It isn't sidhe or witch magic. And it isn't in the tattoo. Something is keeping your night human side at bay in every cell in your body. Something I don't understand, or can help you with. I'm sorry."

Beck stood up and nodded to Devin. Jax had no clue what they had just done, but it seemed their trip was over and nothing had changed.

"Do you think it's something like mitochondrial DNA?" Cassie asked Devin. She didn't seem to have a problem interrupting Devin with her ideas. "I mean, all the hunters are female and mitochondrial DNA is passed by the females. Just a thought."

Devin nodded at her thought process.

"If I took a little blood I could do some testing," she added, reaching for Jax's hand.

Beck was across the room in a flash. "Sorry, no blood."

Devin nodded at the startled Cassie. "You can take some of mine since we're family," he told her. "Seems I have more than one night human locked inside of me."

Cassie looked shocked at that admission. Now Jax really wondered what passed between the two brothers. Devin seemed to know a lot without Beck's knowledge, but now that they'd shared ideas, he probably knew everything.

"We will contact you if we figure anything out," Devin told Beck as Beck turned to leave.

"As we will to you," Beck replied with a nod to Devin. Without another word, Beck turned to leave. Jax would have liked to be included in their conversation, heck he just wanted to be able to ask a few more questions, but it seemed their time was done.

Jax had no choice but to follow Beck out of the sidhe village and back home. They were running out of time and had just hit another dead end. While it seemed his problem of controlling his night human side was now fixed—at least he hoped it was—they were no closer to saving Simone.

CHAPTER 7

Jax **stared at** the ceiling of his bedroom. He had been awake for a while, but couldn't get himself out of bed. It was nice to be able to use his night human powers again in day human form without going crazy, but it didn't solve anything. They had spent nine hours driving to meet Devin and nine hours driving home, wasting a complete day without getting the answer they were looking for, and Simone was only getting worse.

"Are you sure it worked?" Jen asked as she popped her head through the hole between the rooms he had made before he left. "You're not going to make this a doorway now?"

Jax rolled his eyes at her.

"If it really worked, maybe I should go visit the witch," Jen suggested.

"Beck said she replaced the seal. She didn't make a new one, I guess," Jax replied. He had asked the same thing on his way home. The whole brotherly bonding thing with his perfect brothers gave Beck more answers that he probably wouldn't share, but at least he had spoken more than on the ride there, and had even answered a few of Jax's questions. Jax was careful enough not to ask about how it felt to see his brother after so long.

"What's the plan now?" Jen asked.

"There is no plan," Jax admitted defeat.

Beck and Jax had brainstormed little on the nine-hour ride back. They didn't have any other options, and it seemed that they were running out of time. Wes was giving Simone less than a week before the cancer would kill her. Beck advised Jax to make his farewells and accept that there were some things you just can't change.

"Come on. There's always a plan," Jen replied. "You can't just give up."

"It's not that I want to." Jax was relieved to see his anger wasn't flaring up. The spell Cassie had used worked really well. All he felt now was sadness. "It's that I don't know enough to even guess what to do next. I feel so lost. Here I was, raised to hunt night humans but know so little about everything. Beck makes it all seem easy, like he was born to be a night human. I was born into the world and know nothing. I really thought it was the tattoo."

"Well, it wasn't. Now move on and keep thinking." Jen sure made a good motivational speaker.

Jax covered his face with his arms. He had been thinking. Nine hours in the car ride home he had contemplated everything. Nothing more was coming to mind. How could he fix something if it was like Cassie had guessed—in his DNA? He wasn't a scientist.

"Now think about it. Beck isn't a day human full time. Why is that? The magic can be broken. He's proof. So don't give up. Don't give up on Simone."

Jax didn't want to look at Jen. She was becoming exasperating with all her positive talk. It wasn't like he was sitting around playing video games and not trying. They had driven off to almost both sides of the country in less than a week and still hadn't found any answers. Their all-knowing father didn't even have answers, and he was older than dirt. How the heck was Jax supposed to figure it out? The only ones with answers were the hunters, and they weren't speaking with him right now.

"Okay, it sucks that everything isn't working, but you know there's an answer. Someone has to know," Jen continued her motivational tirade. "You just aren't talking to the right person yet."

Taking his hands off his face, Jax looked at his thoughtful sister to see the hole in the wall. She was good. That was it, wasn't it? He needed to talk to the right person, and he had a clue who the right person was. There was one last option he hadn't tried yet. While the hunters weren't speaking to him, there was one, in particular, he was pretty sure would. At least he hoped she would.

Jen took a deep breath to continue her lecture as Jax sat up on the bed. He reached through the hole, pushing her back and bumping the picture on her side back into place in front of her face to divide their two rooms again.

"B-but ..." she sputtered.

"Thanks, sis. I got an idea who to call now. Someday I hope I can introduce you to her, too. You'd like her."

Jax stood and grabbed his phone before heading outside to be alone. He needed privacy for this conversation and was hoping to finally find the answer he was seeking. Time was almost out. While the other hunters wouldn't talk to him, he was pretty sure Jade still would. And he knew she couldn't turn down helping Simone. Now if she could only find the answer, they could both save their friend together.

Finding the quietest spot he knew of on the property, Jax climbed up into the nearest tree. The old grove had many trees to pick from, but the one he chose was easy enough to climb and still be up out of sight. He needed to be alone if it turned out Jade was too much a hunter to care about him now. He hadn't thought about his call to her only days ago was possibly sealing his fate from ever going back or that she would then be forbidden to talk to him. He really wasn't sure if it would work, but he hoped that his bond with Jade was strong enough that she would answer. If JoAnne was correct, he had been disowned. That would mean none of the hunters could speak with him, including his sister.

Calling Jade was his last hope. Taking a deep breath, he pressed the number for his sister. He was happy that it was daytime and his chances of being interrupted were slim. He didn't need anyone hearing the rejection if Jade didn't take the call, nor did he need anyone to see if the seal that Cassie had put on him broke as he guessed it might if he completely lost it. This was his last hope.

The phone rang once. No pickup. It rang again. Again, no answer. Jax was a little worried. Jade was pretty good at answering her phone since she was always on it. It rang a third time, and Jax knew what that meant. It would be going to voice mail. It seemed that Jade was a hunter more than a sister after all. Jax stared at the screen of his phone and hung up without leaving a message. It stunk to know where he stood, but it was reality. He had left the hunters. He hadn't thought they'd disown him so fast, but it didn't surprise him too much. Males meant nothing in the hunter world.

Leaning back, Jax closed his eyes and let the sunshine peeking from between the trees warm him. He took a deep breath and attempted to settle the anger and sadness that was engulfing him. It would be nice if he had some sort of night human power that could wish him away and make everything all better. Cassie was the closest he had seen to magic, but even that was limited. He could tell what she did took time and study. He wanted a natural gift that would let him forget his life, maybe even let him start a new one.

There was no way possible he would be able to face Simone. He had failed. He hadn't been able to save her a second time. Once was bad enough, but twice was unforgivable. She would die hating him. It was hard enough to admit to himself that he didn't deserve to see her.

Everything about his life stunk. He knew the truth now, but it didn't matter. It wasn't a truth he wanted. He was heir to being a blood-sucking monster. His sister had disowned him. The people he had called family his whole life just abandoned him. He had found his first crush a second time, and when she needed him, he had failed. Nothing in his life was good. He wanted to go back and be born into a non-complicated life where it wasn't screwed up like his. He wanted an out, and there wasn't one.

Jax wasn't sure what to do next. He was positive the hunters didn't want him back, and not so sure where he would stay with the vampyre for that matter. He was the heir, but what good was he if he wasn't a night human? He was pretty sure Wes was banking on him being part of the family in every way. Jax was just a human. He wasn't what they wanted or needed. So would he be on his own? Beck made it sound like Jax would be hunted for who his father was, but if he was just a human, no one would care. His blood held the same power as every other hunter out there and nothing more. Jax wasn't the heir they needed, nor what anyone would want without a night human side. It wasn't that Jax wanted to be a night human, but without it, he couldn't save Simone. And he wouldn't be needed. Jax came to New Orleans to find himself. He had found a father and a new life, but he wasn't sure about anything anymore.

The phone in his hand rung, and Jax stared at it in shock. Jade was calling him back.

"Hello," he quickly said as he fumbled with the buttons to get her before she hung up.

"Hey, bro, how's it going?" Jade asked.

"Wasn't sure you were allowed to talk to me," Jax replied. He really was worried, but tried not to let it into his voice.

"For now it's fine," she stated. "Mom said you're on a find yourself mission like most of the males take at some point."

"Find myself?" Jax almost laughed at how she put it. Rommy wasn't the type to tell tales. In fact, he found that if she didn't want to answer, she usually didn't. Her little lie was quite funny to Jax.

"The hunters all think you'll be back soon," Jade added, sounding a bit hopeful.

That wasn't happening. He wasn't going to go back to being a second-class citizen. He was pretty sure there was no life left for him with the hunters no matter what came next.

"Because I know the truth of who our father is," Jax deduced. The hunters did their best to raise him to hate night humans, and he had a feeling it wasn't just because they hunted them. It was probably a way to get the sons to reject their fathers.

"Yeah, about that ..."

"I take it they haven't told you yet?" Of course, they hadn't told her, and he wasn't going to be the one to drop that bombshell. That was all on Rommy. She could have the fun of explaining that.

"Told me what?"

Jax smiled. He missed Jade. Like, really missed her. They had spent their whole lives, only the two of them. Their mother was around, but she wasn't very motherly or even family-oriented for that matter. If Jax needed someone, it was Jade he could depend on. Heck, that was why he was calling her right now. Maybe someday she would need him. That would be nice, but for now, it was just the normal. Jax, the little brother, needed Jade, his older sister.

"The truth about our parents. And before you even ask, I'm not telling you. Mom can have the fun of letting that out. And maybe I should give you my address for when she does, so you can come join me." Jax doubted she would leave the hunters—hunting was her whole life—but she was going to be mad.

"Come on, our dad can't be that bad if you're staying there longer. What? Is he old, fat, and bald? Maybe tells all those really bad dad jokes. He can't be a complete loser if Mom actually loved him at some point."

Jax chuckled. Oh, he was bad in hunter terms and then some, but not in the way Jade was ever going to guess.

"Jax, don't make me come there and beat it out of you," Jade threatened.

Jax smiled to himself. He loved when she threatened him. Yes, she was older by almost one year, and she was stronger, but she wasn't bigger, and with night human blood that he now had access to, he might be able to take her for once.

"I'd love to visit with you, and as fun as it is knowing something you don't, I actually have something else to talk about with you," Jax said, changing the subject.

Jade huffed. She didn't let go easily.

"Remember the old games we used to play?"

"Mm-hmm," Jade replied. She had to guess where Jax was going.

"We have a red enemy we haven't seen for a long time that I found recently. We thought the red enemy was gone but turns out not."

Jax paused to see if Jade caught on. When they were kids, they discovered that all the hunters talked and reported back to Rommy. There wasn't a single thing they could get away with if they were in hunter territory because someone was always lurking in the shadows and reporting back. Jade and Jax had to devise a language just for themselves to understand and they called it their code. It was actually quite simple. They would talk as normal but put a color in front of a word that was meant to be the opposite. Sometimes the meaning got confusing when you had to guess the opposite, but most of the time it worked.

"Did we think the red enemy was dead?" Jade asked cautiously.

"For a little bit," Jax answered. "It took us a while, but we found that they weren't really dead."

"Is this just something you've heard or seen with your own eyes?"

"I've seen the red enemy and talked to them."

Jade gasped on the other end of the line. Jax knew that she understood exactly who he was talking about.

"There's more," Jax added before she could ask more questions. "The red enemy is yellow healthy. Like think sunny, sunny yellow. So yellow healthy, they can't come home."

"So what can we do?"

"That's why I've called you. I've tried and tried to figure things out on my own, but I can't seem to find the answer. I even visited our green land friends to get help. And they said to tell you hi."

"How can I help? Should I leave tonight, bring anyone with?" Jade sounded worried now. He knew that she understood how bad it was, but that wasn't an answer.

"Actually, you can't come to see them. The red enemy can't be found by their family, and you don't even want to know where I found them."

"But what can we do. I don't want them ..." Jade didn't finish, and Jax didn't blame her. He didn't want Simone to die, either. That's why he was traversing the country, searching for answers.

"Neither do I. That's why I need you to look into someone for me. I need you to look closer at hunters' black death. I mean, I know all about cemeteries and burials and all. But that's just it. I know where we end up, but I don't know the details." Jax hoped that got across to her.

"What about black death?" Jade asked.

"That's just it; I don't know. No one knows. There are so many details Mom hasn't shared with you yet, but this is one they don't share with anyone until just before it happens. Something essential to hunters' black death and not to anyone else."

"Well, it must not be parentage, since you've already met our father and you know the basics of how it's done. But what more is there to know?" Jade sounded confused, and he knew she would be. It would have been easier if they were ever truly alone. And if Jade knew the truth, she might be able to grasp the rest, but they didn't have time for that either.

"If you find out as much as you can, I'll meet you at our favorite hangout," Jax told her.

"But that's—" Jade replied.

"And don't worry about it. I'll be there by normal pink lunchtime."

"Sounds good. I'll see you then."

Jax nodded as Jade hung up. He wasn't sure if Jade could find out anything, but even if she led to another idea, it would be worth it. Now he just needed to drive six more hours. What was six more hours in the car after his past two trips?

Hopping from the tree, Jax made his way back to his father's place to grab a bag and get on his way. It was a six and a half hour drive, and to make it there by midnight he'd have to leave soon. Jax thought about finding Beck, but something told him their older brother wouldn't be welcome in his hunter hometown. Actually, no night humans were ever welcomed there. Jax only grabbed a couple sticks of his father's blood for emergencies, like if he ran into other night humans and had to fight back. He'd have to be sure not to use it until after he met with Jade.

Back in his room, Jax peeked through the hole in his wall to Jen's room.

"Hey, Jen," Jax said quietly.

He looked inside, but she was gone. He was going to ask her to cover for him, but maybe it was better she didn't know he was leaving. Jax had yet to be able to gauge how Wes would react to something like that. He seemed to demand complete submission from all his vampyre, but Jen wasn't one of them. Jax kind of wondered why she even stuck around.

Without another thought, Jax hurried out of the house before anyone could see and stop him. He needed to meet Jade, and he had to be alone. It didn't matter what rules his father had put in place, Jax needed an answer and one he hoped his hunter sister could find.

Driving over the speed limit the whole way there, Jax got to the playground early. He pulled his motorcycle to a stop and parked it where he could make an easy getaway if needed. He was pretty certain the hunters wouldn't kick him out since his mother lied for him, but he wasn't completely sure. He knew their secret now.

Walking over to the park shelter, Jax casually scanned the area for anyone who might be following him. It would have been easier to take a bit of his father's blood, and he would be able to smell people for miles, but he knew that wasn't possible. The hunters didn't allow night humans in their area, and Jax was right in the middle of it at a playground he spent a lot of time at with Jade while growing up.

It was dark out, being that it was almost midnight, but not dark enough that Jax couldn't see. He was likely alone, as long as there wasn't anyone following Jade. Jax walked into the bathroom and made his way over to the back wall. He pushed off the edges of the utility door, and it easily popped open. The lock was fake, and when Jade and Jax had discovered that as kids, they found it the perfect place to hide since you could access the closet from both sides. Jax fixed his side of the door and put the bar over it to stop anyone from entering. Okay, it wasn't going to stop a hunter from entering—they all had super strength—but it would slow one down long enough for Jade and Jax to leave through the other door.

Leaning back against the wall, Jax stared at the door that went into the women's bathroom. He was early, but he was worried just a tad bit that Jade wasn't going to show. If their mother knew they were meeting Jade would be in more trouble than Jax ever wanted her to be in. She might be his older sister, but Jax worried about her. Jade was really all he had before meeting the other side of their family, and even now he wasn't sure about them. There was just something about Wes that made Jax worry. He was a night human and night humans couldn't be trusted. And he was an old night human. You didn't live that long by being nice.

The wall slid a little, and Jax stood quickly. He needed to be ready to leave if it wasn't Jade. He saw the pink spikes of her hair first as she ducked into the room, and that was enough to make him relax.

"New color?" he asked as he sat back down.

Jade shrugged as she turned to secure her door also.

"Do you know how much trouble you'd be in for coming back without telling Mom? She's furious with you, but I think she's actually worried," Jade whispered to him.

Jax smiled. Sure, the famed hunter Rommy was worried, but he doubted it had to do with him being gone. He'd bet she was more concerned over the fact that he now knew the truth and could tell Jade at any moment. Jax had a feeling that most hunters were in their twenties or older when they joined up full time because it was easier to break the news to them about how they would have to have a family. Jade wasn't anywhere near wanting kids. Rommy didn't have anything to worry about her asking, and Jax wasn't going to be the one to have that fun conversation.

"So I did as you asked. I went snooping and looked

into everything I could find. It was actually very confusing. There was all this stuff about night human blood. I'm beginning to think I don't want to know how they're made after all." Jade gagged. She was better at liking the nice night humans which was more than likely thanks to Whitney, but she still didn't like them enough to have kids with one.

"I'm looking for something very specific," Jax replied.

"Not out loud," a voice from above them said.

Jade didn't hesitate to throw a knife at the person speaking. Jax had already moved beside her so they could face the person together. Jax could only think of one person that would be able to find their secret meeting place, and he didn't really want to deal with their mother right now. He was pretty certain she would never help him find the answer he needed as she hated night humans more than most.

The person dropped down to the ground to face Jade and Jax as they both now had weapons in their hands.

Once Jax could see who it was, he lowered his knife and rolled his eyes. Jade didn't move from her stance, ready to attack.

"Jade. It's fine. This is Beck," Jax told her, but she still didn't move. "He's our older brother and acts like a puppy that needs to follow me everywhere."

Beck smiled at Jade, but Jax didn't miss the glare he shot his way first. Jax shrugged. Beck hadn't been invited. He was lucky he had only called him a dog and didn't reveal the rest of the secret about him. Jax was pretty sure Jade would haul off and attack without question if she knew he was a night human.

"Brother?" Jade asked, lowering her knife only slightly.

"And cousin," Beck added with a big smile for her.

"And cousin?" Jade glanced at Jax.

"Our dad had two sons with our mother's older sister before he met mom. Hence, our brother and cousin all rolled into one," Jax explained. He really didn't have time to get into that one and would have to thank Beck later for adding it into the conversation. "And he had one more after me. We have a sister back in New Orleans, and we're the only family she has left."

Jade's eyes bugged at the news. They went from being just the two of them to a group in less than a second. Jax understood how confusing that news was, but it was also good news. Jade and Jax had hoped their whole life for more family. They had even asked about aunts and uncles, but their mother said they were all dead. That much was true. Their aunt was dead, but her children weren't.

"And one more thing," Beck added. "I'm not human."

Jax jumped in front of Beck, taking the swing that he already knew would come from Jade. The knife lodged into his forearm all the way down to the bone. Jax gritted his teeth and was really going to have to save his anger to give Beck later. Was he an idiot? What night human thought it was safe to tell a wary hunter he was a night human? Yeah, his stupid older brother.

"Stop," Jax cried as he threw himself at her with the knife still lodged in his arm. He wrapped his arms around Jade before she could move around him to get to Beck, who was no longer there, of course. Jade bucked him back and was scanning around the small closet. How was it possible that Beck could disappear?

Jax felt the hand on him before he sensed Beck.

'*Stop it,*' Beck commanded, holding Jax and Jade in place. He was in their minds.

"You aren't welcome here," Jade spat out, not happy that she couldn't move.

'*And I wouldn't be here except for our brother running off and not letting me ask for a neutral place to meet. I would have planned this better,*' Beck replied. '*We have to make this quick before the other hunters feel my night human side. I can't shield it longer than a few minutes.*'

Jax would have laughed if he wasn't confused how Beck was talking to both him and Jade mentally. And he was curious about the whole shielding thing, but that was a conversation for another time.

'*Explain quickly, Jax, because I have a feeling she wouldn't believe a word from me,*' Beck ordered Jax.

'*Without getting into details, we need to know how to break the seal placed on us at birth,*' Jax told Jade, who was still eyeing Beck and looking for a way to get to him. '*We have night human blood in us that's sealed away when we are born. That seal is the only thing that can save Simone. If it stays in place, she will die.*'

'*You really found her?*' Jade asked, the fight leeching from her.

'*Yes, and she's dying from cancer. She needs to access the night human blood to heal. We've searched for answers everywhere, but we can't find out how the hunters seal the night human side. No one seems to know.*'

Jade looked at Jax as her face fell. '*Then I can't help. I never found anything about sealing night human blood.'*

'It might not have said that,' Beck interrupted and earned himself a glare from Jade. *'We need to know exactly what the hunters tell people about our births.'*

Then it hit Jade. If Beck was their brother and cousin, then he should be a hunter also. Hunters couldn't be turned into night humans. Beck and Jax got the drift of her thoughts as she stared at Beck in confusion.

'Long story for another time,' Beck told her. *'And I honestly don't even know the why behind it entirely myself. What we need to know right now is how to save Simone.'*

Jax tried not to think anything more about what Beck was saying. If Jade's thoughts could filter across the bond, then so could his. He didn't need Jade finding out the truth. He really didn't need her to know how bad it was for Simone.

'What exactly did you read about hunter births? Did anything seem out of place?' Beck kept Jade focused.

'I did read about night human blood being involved, but they didn't say how it was added to the baby or why. There really wasn't much. Everything I found seemed normal enough. Baby comes out. Wash and bathe the baby. Present it to the elders to be kissed by the fey. You know, the normal stuff,' Jade explained.

Jax tried not to be disappointed. She had tried, and he hadn't given her more to go on.

'Kissed by the fey?' Beck asked.

Jade shared a look with Jax as if to ask if Beck was really related.

'It's a hunter thing. When you're growing up, and you realize that you're stronger, faster, and heal better than normal

kids and you ask your mother about it, she always says that you were kissed by the fey.'

'Not literally,' Jax continued as Beck looked at *them like they were speaking in a different language. 'Like how kids think the boogeyman lives under the bed. It's just made up as a reason we have powers because they can't explain it to us, or sometimes I wondered if they just didn't know.'*

Beck let go of Jade and Jax. She stared at him, and Jax realized he was back to being a normal human. He had grown so used to Beck that he didn't even notice as their older brother changed from one form to the other.

"Not possible," she whispered.

"Oh, Beck is all sorts of not possible," Jax replied.

"Stay in here a little longer before leaving. You don't want to be seen with me," Beck explained as he made his way to the door that was still barricaded shut to the men's bathroom.

"What difference does it make? You're human now," Jax asked.

"Most won't know the difference, but if your mother comes looking, she will," Beck answered. "And the last time I spoke with her, years ago, I promised to never speak with Jade. So I kind of just broke a promise to the hunter extraordinaire that would love nothing more than a reason to pick a fight with me. I'd hate to have to take her down. She does actually make my job easier."

"And she's your aunt and all," Jade added. Beck just shrugged.

And with that, Beck was gone.

"Is he really?" Jade asked in a whisper.

Jax nodded. "And the funny part is he's a hunter, too.

There's a whole group of night humans that hunt bad night humans."

Jade's eyes bugged, and Jax smiled. Without missing a beat, he reached forward and hugged her. He was sure her eyes would be coming out of her head by now. It had been years since he had hugged her. But then again, he wasn't sure when he would see her again, if ever. He wasn't coming back to the hunters.

They weren't a hugging family, but Jax understood better now. Beck had shown him that. They never wanted to say good-bye. Each and every day fighting was a day their lives were on the line. The hunters dealt with loss all the time, so they didn't get attached. It was easier to bury someone if you already expected them to die. Jax wasn't going to lie to himself any longer. He was attached. He loved his sister. He should have never left home the first time without finding her first. She was his best friend and sister all packaged into one. She deserved a proper good-bye.

And Jax knew what he needed to do. Simone didn't deserve to die alone. Her parents were wrong to leave her behind. He didn't save her in the end, but he could be there for her. He needed to go back and be with her. She wasn't alone and wouldn't be forgotten.

"Thanks for trying to help," Jax added as he stepped back to leave the same way as Beck.

"Is she really dying?"

"Yes. And I need to get back to her. She has less than a week left. I've tried everything, but there isn't an answer. I'm guessing even the hunters don't know. And the blood that is locked away was the last chance. It is lost with whoever made it happen, so yes, she is dying."

This time Jax was surprised when Jade hugged him. "Tell her this one was from me."

Jax pushed the door back to leave. He smiled at Jade and nodded. It had to be killing Jade to not see her friend, but life was what it was. Jade was a hunter, and while Jax could be forgiven for going to find his father, Jade wouldn't be.

"I'm looking forward to the whole story when you come back someday," Jade said to Jax as he stepped into the men's bathroom. Jax just nodded. She was going to be waiting a long time.

He exited the bathroom and dropped his phone in the trash on his way out. There was no coming back to the hunters and a place he no longer belonged. He was going to go back to Simone, and then to find his own way. No more waiting for others to tell him what to do. It was time to decide for himself.

CHAPTER 8

The ride back to New Orleans was depressing. Jax had tried his last effort to get answers, and had found nothing. Jade couldn't ferret out the answer, and Jax was more than sure his mother would never give it to him, even if she knew. It was likely she didn't know herself, as it sounded like all that Jade could find were old wives' tales. And Jax didn't need tales; he needed facts and answers. He needed to save Simone, and it looked like that wasn't going to happen.

When he finally pulled into his father's place, it only took seconds for Beck to follow behind him. It wasn't like he was hiding from him anymore and he'd spotted him on more than one occasion trailing behind him. Jax left his bike next to the house and went inside to finally get some sleep.

"Jax?" Wes called from the living room.

Jax nodded. He'd have to wait to rest. You didn't keep your clan leader waiting. He'd learned that much about night human politics. For now, he would be the obedient son, but who knew where life was going to take him next.

"Coming," Jax replied as he somberly made his way through the kitchen and into the family room where the older night human waited.

"Jade didn't have the answer?" Wes asked.

"No. I really thought she'd find something. Simone means as much to her as she does to me, but turns out there was nothing but old stories and legends. The hunters don't even mention a seal or anything. It's like they don't even know."

Jax sat down across from his father. He knew what was coming next. He had ran off without permission. Now it was time for punishment.

"What did she say?" Wes asked.

Well, that wasn't what Jax was expecting. He was expecting his father to issue an order that forbade him from ever leaving the house, and he'd have to do exactly what the old man said because his word was law if he commanded something. As long as Jax was part of the family, it seemed he couldn't disobey his father.

"She said that it was all normal stuff beyond not understanding all the references to night human blood which I assume was your contribution to the whole part."

"You didn't tell her who I was?"

"Not a chance. I'm going to let Rommy do that. I only wish I was there to see it." And he really did. Jade was going to be mad once she figured out Rommy wasn't joking, not that their mother joked much. It was going to be epic, but Jax couldn't be there for it when he wasn't going back.

"How kind of you," Wes replied with a wink. He understood and probably wanted to see it himself. "Did Jade mention anything about night humans at all?"

"No." Jax was just as lost as his father. There was nothing more to find.

"She mentioned 'kissed by the fey'," Beck said from the kitchen doorway. He had a bag of blood in his hands that he was opening for a drink. Jax tried not to do a double take. It was easy to pretend his older brother was just another hunter, but while he drank blood, there was no pretending.

Wes' head snapped up as he looked at Beck. It was like they were silently conversing before Wes stood up and nodded. Okay, they probably were silently conversing. It seemed as head of the family, Wes could go into anyone's head at any time. Jax really didn't like that, but it was even more annoying when they had conversations without him. Maybe this was his punishment. Wes and Beck were deciding what to do with him without him knowing.

"You are forbidden to leave the city. That's an order," Wes told Jax. Jax didn't need the last part, because he could feel the weight behind his father's words. He wasn't going to be going anywhere until he said otherwise, even if he wanted to. "I have to go check my contacts."

Wes was gone as quickly as Beck could leave. In his place, Beck sat before Jax.

"If you ever put me in that position again, I don't care what Wes will do to me. I'm not going to take the fall for your stupidity. If the hunters had known you were there, they could have taken you. They don't let the males leave twice. You would be stuck doing what they wanted or exterminated because you knew too much. Even worse, if they had discovered Jade was meeting you on purpose, you would have put her in danger. You might have been allowed to do whatever you wanted with your mother, but know that I was always there keeping you safe. You didn't get out of trouble again and again just because of your skills." Beck glared at Jax as he stood, challenging him to contradict him.

Jax nodded, and Beck left. He wasn't sure, but somehow he'd always known there was someone watching over them when they ran amok. He just didn't know it had been Beck. He owed him a thanks, but that wasn't coming any time soon. Jax hated being told what to do, and right now Beck and Wes were ordering him around. He'd do as Wes ordered, but mainly because their father's word was law. It wasn't like Jax could leave anyway. And he didn't want to leave at the moment, because Simone was still there. He had somewhere to be, and that's where he would be in the morning, as soon as he got a couple hours of sleep.

Jax stood outside Simone's bedroom and tried to calm his nerves. This wasn't how he wanted things to go down. He wanted to sweep in and tell her good news, not bad news. He wanted to be the hero of her story and not the failure he really was. He wasn't even sure how he supposed to tell her she was going to die after all he promised.

"She won't be awake much longer before she needs to rest again," the female vampyre taking care of Simone said from beside Jax.

Taking a deep breath, Jax pushed open the door. Simone was in bed and looked like she was already asleep. He paused in the doorway, wondering if he should enter. Her eyes fluttered open, though, and Jax entered the room.

"You're home." She smiled at him. Even her eyes crinkled with happiness to see him. It was more than a little heart-wrenching. "How long before you leave again?"

"Not sure," Jax replied as he sat on the edge of the bed. He still needed to work up the nerve to tell her the truth about his travels, but he could otherwise share. "I've been put on house arrest."

"Oh, no. What'd you do this time?"

She was genuinely happy to see him. He couldn't give her bad news.

"I went to see Jade without telling anyone."

"Oh. I bet that didn't go over very well. The prince of the vampyre leaves without notice or his protection entourage. Wes must have been mad. Too bad I sleep too much, or I probably could have heard the yelling from that one. Yeah, I can see how that would lead to house arrest. So how is Jade?"

"Good for now. My mom hasn't told her the truth about night human mates yet. I don't know how she's going to take that one. Luckily some of the younger hunter girls are friends with her now, so she'll have someone to turn to when she finds out."

Simone nodded and closed her eyes. "She is not going to take that well. I know back then I wouldn't have either, but they aren't that bad once you get to know them. Yes, the drinking blood thing is gross, but that doesn't make them bad people. It is still surreal that we'll both be one soon," Simone added with her eyes still closed.

"We didn't find the answer," Jax blurted out. It was easier to do without her looking at him with that hopeful expression on her face.

Simone opened her eyes, and Jax dreaded the look he was going to see. Anger, sadness, refusal to be his friend. But it never came. She was still serenely happy.

"Guess I don't have to worry about that drinking blood thing. Thanks for trying. I know how much you tried. It was more than anyone's ever done for me. So thank you. Guess we can't change fate after all."

She closed her eyes again. He could hear her breathing slow down. He waited, watching to see if her eyes opened or if she had more to say. Just silence.

"She's asleep again," the vampyre told him as she came into the room and tucked the covers tighter around her.

"For how long?" That wasn't as bad as he thought it would be, but seeing her only talk a little and fall back asleep was a reality hit.

"Probably an hour or two." The vampyre finished tucking Simone in and left the room.

Jax moved over and sat beside her on the large bed. She already had lost enough weight to look years younger, and the large bed just accentuated it. Jax picked up her small, thin hand. She was withering away to nothing, and he had failed. He would do now what Beck had said all along. He would be there for her.

Simone had always been different than most of the hunters. Maybe that was why he had been attracted to her. She cared more than the rest of them, and to have her thank him when he failed was just awe-inspiring. He didn't know a single other person that would be grateful when dying, but then again, all the death he had seen in the hunter world came in combat. Hunters didn't go quietly into death. At least hunters that weren't Simone.

In fact, the more he thought about it, the more he realized that there was a lot about the hunters he didn't fit in with. It wasn't just that he realized there were good and bad night humans. It was everything. He could never be the cold-hearted killer they wanted from him. He always needed to be sure they were really bad night humans. And in reality, he didn't enjoy getting punched around during practice, or the multiple broken bones he'd received, mainly from his mother. The hunter females thrived on it. Jax just trained because he wanted to keep Jade safe, and that was it. His whole life was centered on keeping Jade safe. Now that he was likely to never see her again, it was time to figure out where he wanted his life to go. And he still didn't have an answer.

Simone stirred a little and Jax leaned over to brush the hair out of her face. She murmured something and went back to restful sleep.

Jax wasn't sure what options he had. For now, he had to obey his father, and he was sure Beck wasn't going to let him out of his sight. But once everything was settled with Simone, Jax would have to choose what to do. While he said he'd be his father's heir, he couldn't be without being a night human first. He was a reject. His father would have to find another heir, because there was nothing Jax could do about it even if he wanted to be a night human. And he realized, as he watched Simone sleep, there was nothing he wanted more at the moment. Being a night human would save her.

The hunters wouldn't welcome him back. Beck was right to be afraid of his impromptu visit with Jade. He agreed that it was likely that the hunters would lock him away, or maybe even kill him for betraying them. Taking night human blood to increase your strength was against the rules, and cohabiting with them was grounds for death. Jax was screwed there, too, and Beck didn't even know those rules.

And that was just it. He could go back and possibly be locked away by the hunters or continue the madness of searching for a way to join the vampyre, which he wasn't sure he'd want to do once Simone was gone. Jax didn't have a third option. What else could he do with his life? He had a high school diploma, but no aspirations to do anything. He had been raised his whole life to fight night humans. That was supposed to be his life. Without that as a job, what else was he good at?

Jax watched Simone sleep. She looked peaceful. He felt so bad that he couldn't help her. He had tried, and it hadn't been enough. A soft ping from the attached bathroom brought Jax's attention away from Simone. He moved to go see what it was at the same time his father entered the room. Jax froze where he was in the middle of the room—something was going on, and he didn't want to leave Simone unprotected.

"Glad to see we found you here," he told Jax, as if Jax had many options. After his little escape to visit Jade before, he now couldn't even attempt to leave as the command behind his father's voice ordered him to stay in the city.

"We?" Jax turned back to the bathroom.

From the bathroom came a small child. Well, she was the size of a small child, but upon further inspection, it turned out that she wasn't one at all. She was the height of a child, but that was it. She was a perfectly formed female, all in green, just a miniature version. Her forest-green eyes looked at Jax, and then Simone.

"Hunter children," she said in a shrill voice that matched her small size.

The green lady waited a moment as if she was being cautious of Jax before moving. Her green hair—which matched her green eyes, skin, and leaves that kept her modestly clad— flipped over her shoulder as she walked closer.

"You," she pointed a finger at Wes as she turned suddenly, "old night human, need to go away." She gave him a smile, but there was nothing friendly behind it. With a wave of her tiny green hand, Wes disappeared in a pop just like the sound Jax had heard the moment before.

"Where'd he go?" Jax asked cautiously. If the green lady was making people disappear, he'd rather be prepared for wherever he would end up.

"I just sent him home where he can't eavesdrop. The old vampyre might have been able to find me and trick me into coming here, but he doesn't get to stick around for this. The magic he asked me to perform is between me and you. He has no place having this knowledge."

"Magic? Who are you?" Knowledge? Jax had no idea what was going on. There was no sharing of knowledge.

And if she was going to do magic, Jax would be even more lost. He wasn't a witch.

Jax was truly confused. He had a feeling she was a night human, the green skin kind of gave her away, but he didn't know what kind. He wracked his brain for some sort of memories from his studies. She didn't look like anything he had seen or even read about before. He could remember a few green-tinged night humans, but none that were all green like her or any that were tiny. She looked like a normal person, just smaller. Night humans came in all shapes and sizes, but he would have remembered a tiny green one in his studies.

"I'm Essie, the fifth and last of my kind."

Which is? Jax wanted to ask, but he kept his mouth shut. He didn't want to go up in a cloud of smoke and leave Simone alone with the weird lady. Jax's lack of response didn't seem to matter as the green lady smiled, much kinder than she had when she poofed his father out of the room.

"I'm a fey."

Fey weren't real. They were made up. Sprites that helped the good and punished the bad little hunters. There had to be some way to control the children who were stronger and faster than their peers. How in the world could she be something made up to keep children in line? She smiled again, and this time Jax could see the perfectly razor-sharp teeth in her mouth. She was certainly a night human. In fact, it seemed all her teeth were pointed, not just the incisors like most night humans. He wasn't going to get too close to her.

Hunters had often talked about the fey, but not as

night humans. They were treated with benevolence and fear, and on occasion with malice. If there was a bad hunt, some would say it was the curse of the fey, others would say they hadn't asked the fey for help, but no one had ever seen a fey. They were like magical, non-existent beings that gave hunters magic when they were young and protected them during fights. He had to be sure if they were real, he would have been told that in his lessons. In fact, it might have been more effective to have one show up and actually punish a child if that was really what the green lady was.

"But fey aren't real." Jax just couldn't help that one thought had slipped out.

And then Jax wanted to smack himself in the head for his own stupidity. Of everything he had seen in the past couple years, he had to know "doesn't exist" was code for it does exist. Mermaids weren't real, and certainly, Oceanids weren't, but Whitney was, and she had a tail. Vampyre were thought to be extinct, but they weren't. And the list could go on and on. The hunters might keep the bad night humans in line, but they certainly didn't know everything.

The little fey woman just continued to smile as Jax was lost in his thoughts, almost as if she were listening in. She nodded her tiny little head. That would be crazy. He knew clan leaders had that ability, but not cross species. However, her smile said otherwise. He had a feeling she could hear his every thought.

"I can."

That proved it. Maybe it was a dream. He could have fallen asleep next to Simone. Jax went to pinch his own arm. It didn't wake him up, and of course, that never worked in real life. Maybe he needed to think of something even more outrageous, so it would confirm his suspicions.

"This is no dream, child. I'm really here, and I'm here to help her." The fey, Essie, pointed at Simone. "You have been correct all along, even if you didn't know why. This hunter child is dying, and the only way to save her is by removing the hunter curse put upon her."

"Curse?" They had all thought it was a seal to keep the hunters human. Curse gave it a whole different meaning.

"Curse," Essie continued. "The fey helped make the night humans, but we weren't naïve enough to think there wouldn't be bad eggs in our creations. To help with that, we created hunters—night humans who would track and keep the bad night humans in line. We gave the hunter line stronger powers, and they were better in every way than their counterparts. This better status led to many disagreements, and when the hunters decided to take on the original creations and began to kill off all we had made, we felt we needed to punish them. We used our magic to seal their night human side. Hunters were turned human, and were no longer stronger and faster than our babies."

That was a lot to process. Jax had never imagined where the hunters came from. When he found out his father was a night human, he agreed that there must be something keeping his night human side away, keeping him human and protecting him. He never imagined it was the opposite; he was being forcibly kept human—it was a curse, not a boon that separated him from his night human side.

"So I should have been a night human all along?"

Essie nodded. "You all should have been. And you should have been stronger, strong enough to rule and lead them."

That was a lot to take in. With the hate hunters had for night humans, he was pretty sure now why that hate came into their culture. They hated what they couldn't be, not that night humans preyed on day humans. They once were those very monsters. And it made complete sense. If you wanted to police night humans, you wouldn't want to use day humans. Jax had seen how much more effective Beck was with his night hunters.

"You created the night humans?" Jax spoke before he realized he had said anything out loud.

"Not me, personally. I'm the youngest left alive. I wasn't around for that, but we have a shared history when we're born, and I know what was done. My kind did indeed create night humans."

"How many are you? I thought you were just fairy tales."

"There are always five of us. When one dies, the next is born to replace them."

Five creatures responsible for all the varied night humans across the world. That seemed amazing at best, but then again, night humans were created centuries ago. His own father was older than dirt.

"You created my father," Jax added.

Smiling, the green lady nodded. "We did, though I would have chosen someone else if I had been around."

Jax wanted to know what that meant, but a sigh from

the bed brought his attention back to why the fey was there to begin with. He'd have to ask how at a later time.

"And you can save Simone?"

"I can, but as with all magic, it comes at a price."

Jax nodded. That much he knew was true.

"What is the price?" Jax needed to know if he could pay it. It was his last attempt to save her.

Essie clapped her hands, and it looked like there was a glitter explosion in Simone's room. Jax watched as glitter fell everywhere, coating not just the room but him, too. He coughed as he breathed some in.

"This is for your ears only. My magic will keep this between us."

Jax leaned in closer. It was like he was getting to hear a great secret.

"The magic that binds the hunter curse wasn't just about keeping your night human side away. It was also at limiting the hunter's procreation. They had grand plans to take over the world. Not only to kick out the original night humans, but also the day humans. They wanted to be supreme. As fey, we don't like to intervene. We wanted to stay out of things, but we couldn't. The hunters were dangerous. We needed to do something, so we limited how many children hunters could have and bound the curse to that."

Jax nodded. That made sense so far. He was following her words, but he wasn't sure where she was going with it.

"If I make her a night human, then her second has to be also."

"Her second?" Nope, Jax didn't understand that one.

"Her sibling, the one carrying the power that holds them both human. When we suppress the night human side, we are only surpassing half of the person. Hunters have to have two children to surpass a whole night human. If I turn this one into a night human, then I turn her second into one also. Hunter children come in pairs to keep the curse active."

"Polly would turn into a night human?"

Simone's younger sister was only twelve. Jax remembered the last time he saw her years ago. She was just a kid. She wasn't even a hunter yet. What would they do with her if that happened? Hunters killed unknown night humans on sight. What would happen if Polly turned into one? Would Simone ever forgive him if he saved her life, but not her sister's?

Jax didn't know what to do. He needed to save Simone, but at what cost? Her life for her sister's didn't seem fair. He needed to find an answer quickly, and his mind was drawing a blank. He had to save her and her sister.

"I can see that you require time," Essie told him. "I will return in two hours to see what you decide." And with another pop, Essie the fey disappeared, taking the glitter with her.

Jax looked at the sleeping Simone and sighed. He wanted to keep her safe, but he didn't want to put Polly in danger. He needed a plan, and quickly. Two hours wasn't much time.

Jax ran back to his father's house from the cottage Simone was staying in. His father had one main house and many smaller ones Jax was still discovering on the property. He slowed when he got closer and could see that his father was standing in the open doorway.

"She left?" he asked. Jax couldn't read the old vampyre's mood.

"For now," Jax replied, still not getting what his father was asking. "Is Beck here?"

"I believe he's at the main house," Wes replied, not moving from the doorway.

Jax paused as he realized his father hadn't just continued to stand in the doorway, but he hadn't moved at all. Wes was very good at sitting still, but his awkward stance made Jax think there was more to it. Jax looked over his father from head to toe and understood more. Correction, he couldn't move at all.

"Is something wrong?" Jax asked cautiously. Wes was the most powerful night human Jax had ever met. Something that bound him like that would be a problem to deal with.

Wes' lip moved into a smile, and that seemed to be all that could move on the old vampyre.

"The fey don't like to be told what to do. I caught her fair and square, but it seems I'm getting a timeout for being a bad boy." Wes wasn't even the slightest upset by his predicament.

Jax nodded. He had a feeling he should be terrified of the small green lady, but he didn't have time to fear what was his last chance to help Simone.

"So she's not really gone," he added, remembering

that Beck had a teammate he'd met and then forgot. Disappearing was a trick, but it didn't mean she had left them.

"Did she tell you that she'll make you a night human?" Wes didn't even care if the fey was around or not.

Jax paused as he had been turning to leave. He hadn't even asked, and now he was worried what that meant. If he wanted to be the night human his father wanted of him, he would have to let Jade turn also, and that would kill her. She didn't even know the truth about the old man, let alone herself.

Jax turned back to his father and wished Beck had taught him how to shield his thoughts, not just how to throw a punch. He had just devolved the fey lady's secret to his father with his thoughts. He was supposed to be the only one that knew about the night human origin, but now his father knew, too. Jax didn't want to think what sort of punishment would be his is if just finding the fey was getting his father a timeout.

Wes stared blankly at Jax.

"Well, did she tell you?" he asked again.

It was odd that he asked again. Yes, she did tell me, Jax thought to himself. Wes seemed to be growing impatient. Wes huffed and looked like he was trying to shake his head.

"She blocked you from me, didn't she?" Wes caught on first.

Jax had no idea what his father meant. Yes, she had coated the room in magic, but it all went with her.

"You can't hear my thoughts?"

"No, otherwise I wouldn't have to ask again."

"She told me she could save Simone, but that was it. We didn't talk about me," Jax replied honestly, in case his father could still sense something.

"Just know that this is your one chance. Finding a fey again will be next to impossible," Wes told Jax from his frozen position. "You have to get her to make you a night human. Otherwise there will be no second time."

Jax nodded and turned to hurry back to the main house. He didn't stop to see who was awake as people were beginning to stir in the house with the sun setting. Wes was lucky it was still sunny outside, so the vampyre were confined to the house and couldn't see him frozen. Jax made his way through the large kitchen and to the basement training room. That was pretty much the only indisputable place to find Beck if he were in the house.

Sure enough, he was pounding away on a punching bag.

"I need you to do me a favor," Jax told Beck. He didn't stop the combination of punch and kicks he was throwing.

Jax was pretty sure that Beck was still mad at him for running away to see Jade without him. He'd have to get over that quickly. Jax had a plan forming, and Beck was needed for it to all work.

"Okay, I'll go on my own," Jax replied and turned to leave. Beck was in front of him before he made it to the stairs.

"You aren't allowed to leave town," Beck told him.

Jax smiled. "Dad's magic over me is temporarily gone. He can't even hear my thoughts."

Beck stared at him like he was lying. He looked him

over from top to bottom before coming back to his face. Beck stared harder.

"There's magic in you," he said.

Jax reached forward and grabbed Beck's hand, not waiting to tell him they needed a silent connection as he used his pocketknife to cut both his and his brother's hand to form a blood bond to communicate in their heads.

'Fey magic,' he told Beck.

'As in the make-believe fey you both said didn't exist?'

'Yes, the make-believe fey is real, and she's coming back soon. I need you to go meet up with Jade, and I need to use your phone to call her. There's a girl that will soon be a night human in the middle of hunter territory if I want to save Simone. I need you and Jade to take her out of there and bring her back here.'

'You do know we don't run a charity, right? Wes took Simone in as a bargaining chip to get you to do what he wanted,' Beck told Jax.

Jax figured as much. He had yet to see a charitable side to Wes. He was all business, but so was every other night human Jax had ever run across. Jax knew how to deal with night humans. He would be all business, too.

'Well, if he wants me to stick around, he's going to have to do things my way a bit. Simone can be saved, but her little sister will also have to be turned into a night human. I have two hours to report back to the fey and let her save Simone,' Jax told him. He hadn't meant to run away from their father, but Jax would do anything to save Simone, even if it meant going against the old vampyre.

'Okay.' Beck replied.

Okay? Beck was just going to do as Jax asked? He

looked his brother over suspiciously. There had to be a catch.

'The first step in getting strong enough to be my brother is to start thinking for yourself. It seems you might be able to surpass me after all. I'm willing to follow your orders as long as you continue to be you, and not the lackey our father wants,' Beck replied. *'Tell Jade to meet me where I first met her. She knows where that is.'*

Beck let go of Jax's hand and handed him his phone.

"I'm going to assume you haven't gotten a new one yet since you threw yours away." Beck was always one step ahead of Jax. Beck opened his phone and logged into it. "There's only one condition to all of this."

There was the Beck Jax was expecting.

"Since you now have new powers, I need reassurance. You can't leave the vampyre grounds until I get back. You're safe here. I can't go running off if I think you won't stay safe."

That Jax could do, and it wasn't like he had plans to go running around anyway.

"I'll stay here," Jax told Beck. But why did Beck care? If he wanted Jax to be free of their father, why did he still want to protect him?

"But why does it matter? Will Wes punish you?" That had to be it. Beck didn't want to be punished.

"Wes has no control over me. I do as he asks because he's smart, but that's it. If I think he's made a stupid choice, I'll do it my way. He certainly isn't my clan leader. I don't belong to a clan. He's my family in blood only, but you, Devin, Jade, and Jen are my family. I'll keep you safe without being ordered to."

Jax stared at Beck. He had only known him for less than a few weeks. How could he feel that strongly?

Beck laughed. "You've been trying to get me to say my age since you first met me, but just know this ... I've watched all four of you grow up. You are my family. Now get to calling Jade, because she still doesn't get that we are family and would hang up immediately if I called."

Jax nodded as he remembered the phone his brother was offering him.

"Good. I'll meet you by the house in two minutes. Make it quick."

Jax took his brother's phone and quickly dialed Jade's number. It was a good thing he had it memorized, and not just on his phone. He waited as it rang, not expecting her to answer. It was going to take a few calls to get her attention with an unknown number. Or maybe not.

"Hello. Who is this?" Jade asked.

"It's me. I'm on our brother's phone," Jax said as he left the main house and began to walk back to his father's house that sat just behind. He paused far enough away so that Wes couldn't listen in.

"You need to go get our red enemy's sibling and get the heck out of town for a little bit," Jax told her. "I can't explain further, but do it now and meet our brother at the place where you first met him. He'll explain more then."

Jax hung up before she could ask questions. He didn't have time to play games or deal with her night human-hating crap that was sure to follow being ordered to meet up with a night human. Beck needed to go and get Polly so that Simone could be saved. Jax walked back to the house, and Beck was waiting in his car with someone in the passenger seat. Jen smiled up at Jax as he neared.

"I figured I could use a bit of help since I'm meeting with girls, or rather a girl that's already tried to kill me more than once," Beck explained as he held out his hand.

Jax put the phone in it. "More than once?"

Beck smiled and drove away. "A story for another time," he called as he disappeared down the long driveway.

"Everything okay?" Wes asked from the doorway, unable to read Jax's mind to know what was going on. Jax kind of liked that new freedom.

"It will be," Jax told him as he turned to go back to Simone's room in the cottage behind the main house. It had to be, because he could finally do something. He was going to save Simone.

CHAPTER 9

Jax sat nervously beside Simone as she slept. He wished he hadn't thrown his phone away and then he could check in with Beck and Jen. It wasn't that he had doubts—Beck wouldn't fail him—but there was nothing more to do as he waited. Jax was nervous more so for his sister. He had asked Jade to abduct a hunter child and run away. If anyone caught her, she would be in trouble. If anyone caught Polly, she would likely be executed as soon as she changed because she'd be a night human and they'd need to preserve their secret.

Jax still couldn't believe that they didn't ever ask questions that would lead them to their father. Sure, they had asked questions, but never once did they look further or even suspect that they had night human blood. None of the hunter kids did. It was probably the best hunter-kept secret in the whole clan. Jade was going to be so upset when she found out, and even more so that Jax knew first.

Simone continued to sleep as Jax sat beside her. Waiting wasn't Jax's forte. He had been able to do it as a hunter on the hunt, but that was exciting. Waiting now wasn't exciting. He was filled with worry from all directions.

What would happen to Simone and would she forgive him that he was making Polly into a night human, too? He hoped she would since he was trying his best to save the young hunter. And then there was Wes to be worried about. His father wanted something Jax couldn't do. He could never change Jade's fate into being a night human. He was going to let the fey go without being able to do what Wes wanted. Where would that leave him then? How would the old night human take it? Jax was about to find out as soon as the green lady returned and did her magic. Then he'd have to face his father and deal with the old man's wrath.

Simone's eyes fluttered open and were a welcome distraction until her breathing began to get labored.

"Simone, it's all right," Jax told her as he reached down and took her hand. It didn't curl into his in response, but just laid there in his own. "I found an answer. We can save you. Just hold on a little longer."

"Jax," she said as she took a deep breath, "you've always been a good friend." She paused again. "Thanks for trying. You don't need to pretend."

Simone closed her eyes once more. Her breaths sounded hard as she took them. She strained to get air into her lungs, and Jax wanted to die in her place. It wasn't fair. They were so close.

"I'm not joking or pretending. I really found an answer." Jax needed to give her hope. It seemed like Simone could die at any time. She needed to change now.

"Essie," Jax called loudly into the room. Wes guessed she was still around, and Jax hoped she was. "Essie," he called a little louder, making Simone open her eyes again.

"My vampyre isn't Essie, and she can't help me now."

Simone paused and took a couple of shallow breaths. "I can feel it. The blood won't work," Simone whispered. Tears were falling from the corner of her eyes. "I'm dying, Jax, and there's nothing more we can do."

"Not yet," Jax pleaded. He needed the fey to come back soon, or it would all be for nothing. All he did, all he tried, it would be for nothing if Simone died. He thought he could sit there and be a good friend as Beck had explained, but he couldn't. Maybe it was the hunter in him that just couldn't give up, but he wasn't going to let her die when they were so close.

"You are correct. It's your hunter side that drives you to keep fighting. It was the only way we could guarantee hunters would be worth the magic it took to make them. We couldn't breed quitters," Essie said as she materialized from nothing.

"We need to do this now," Jax told her as he still held onto Simone's limp hand. Her eyes were closed, but her ragged breathing told Jax she was still awake and alive.

"So you accept that her sister will share her fate?" Essie asked.

Jax sadly nodded. He really didn't want to turn Polly into a night human, but they needed to save Simone. Polly would understand, hopefully, eventually. If Jax could, he would take her place, but he wasn't Simone's brother. He was Jade's brother. Heck, that would make his father happy, but he couldn't change who his parents were. Wes was just going to have to disown him.

The green fey eyed Jax over. "That is a good possibility," she told Jax. He had no idea what she was talking about. "I can see that you are a good child. There is no hunger for power in you. You are different than your father and mother. Let me give you this choice. You may take Polly's place for now. Until she comes of age and her night human powers present, you can be the anchor to Simone's night human."

Jax wasn't sure what to make of the deal. It sounded perfect, but there was always a catch with magic.

The fey smiled, showing off her razor-sharp teeth.

"That is correct. I can make you the anchor for now, but when Polly comes of age, she will turn. I can't stop what she will become. Parentage makes all the difference and something I can't change."

Jax nodded. There were many clans like that in the night human world. They still didn't know who Simone's father was, so it made sense that she could stay human longer, but what Jax didn't understand was how he could take her place for now, or what would happen when Polly did turn into a night human.

"And then I go back to being part human?" Jax asked.

Essie shook her head. "I can't undo the magic that will make you a night human again. If you choose this option, you will stay a night human. When Polly turns, then Jade will also."

Jax sucked in his breath. He didn't exactly want to be a night human. He was sure of that, but it would give Polly time. He could sacrifice himself to give her that time, but could he sacrifice Jade? The fey was asking him to turn his sister into a monster. She would never forgive him for that. She would rather be dead than a monster, and Jax knew that much. Could a few years make the difference? Could he get Jade to understand by then?

"What if I ask to take all the powers split between us to go to only me? Could you take away Jade's hunter and night human sides, and leave her human?"

Essie tapped her chin as she thought. She waved a finger in the air and then went back to thinking.

"No, that wouldn't work. The fey all agree that it would make you too powerful. They are already worried that Simone will be stronger than the rest of her clan. When Polly comes into her night human powers, your hunter side cannot go back to you. It will seek out the half in your sister when the time comes, and she will be left as a night human."

It wasn't what he wanted, nor would it be what Jade wanted, but it was what Polly needed. Jax had to call Jade. There was no way he could make that choice without her input. If only Beck had left his phone. Heck, even Jen could have left her phone. They didn't need two phones. Jax paused as he thought.

"Does it matter which sister?" Could the hunter side in him seek out Jen instead? If she were a hunter, she would be able to control the night human side of her.

The fey's eyes grew large as she smiled at him.

"That I can do."

Jax knew Jade would be upset to become a night human, but if he could give Jen control of a hunter, that would be perfect. If the fey could use Jen, then he could save Simone and not have to sacrifice Jade and her life to do it. It would still mean he would be a night human, but if that was what was needed to save Simone and Jen, he was going for brother of the year.

"Under one condition," Essie continued. "You have to

promise that if we ever call on you to take out Simone or her sister because they go rogue like the last night hunters we created, you will do it."

Jax didn't need to wait to answer that. He knew Simone. She was never going to go crazy and power hungry.

"That's a deal," Jax replied, and the fey snapped her fingers.

Magic surrounded the room like a noose. He felt the tug as it tightened. Without knowing how she'd done it, the fey Essie was now kneeling between Simone and Jax. Her head lowered to Simone before he could stop her. He was afraid with her sharp teeth she could hurt Simone before she could be saved. Jax went to stop the fey when he felt it. His body was frozen in place.

"Don't bite her. She won't survive it." It was silly to order around the being that made all the night humans, but he was sure that the green lady didn't know how fragile Simone was.

"It isn't a bite that is needed here."

Essie leaned down closer to Simone as if she was going to kiss her and stopped mere millimeters from her face. Pushing Simone's mouth open with her tiny fingers, Essie began to suck. A small light, barely visible, came out of Simone. Essie let her go, and Simone flopped limply back on the bed. Jax wanted to see if she was still alive, but he couldn't move. Essie walked over and stood in front of Jax. She was only a little taller than him at her full height while he sat. She dipped her face down, and Jax closed his eyes.

His whole life was going to change. He wasn't exactly

given a choice on the matter, as he was choosing the better of two evils, but it just needed to be. At least he could live with his choice. It might take Jade more time to accept what he was about to become, but he hoped that, in much the way their sibling bond transcended the hunter rules, so would it transcend the way she had been raised. He had a feeling that once she found out the truth of hunters, she would come around.

Jax felt the pull from inside of him. He didn't need to see the mist coming out of his mouth; he felt it in every part of his body. When Devin said the magic was in every cell, he was correct. Of course, perfect brother number two was right. And it wasn't fun. Jax couldn't move as the pain went from one end of his body to the other. He couldn't talk either, or cry out in pain. He was frozen as his life was changing in an instant that felt like forever. As the last tug pulled on him, Jax felt the final piece of his humanity leave him. He could never go back. He was a night human now and forever.

Pushing the last of his stuff off the desk and into the box on the floor, Jax was finished. He was packed and more than ready to leave. Only one last thing to do. It was time to speak to his father.

It had been one week since the fey had visited and changed his life. Surprisingly, it was better than Jax had expected. He was the night human son his father wanted, but Jax had as much control to shift between night and day human as Beck. He wondered if this was because he was like Beck, or if was it because of the link with

Simone and Polly. Either way, Jax was able to still walk in the sunlight like Beck and Wes instead of hiding like the rest of the vampyre. And also like his older brother, Jax didn't have to do as Wes commanded. He was his own free man.

Beck had been true to his word and brought Polly back to New Orleans. The sisters were more than overjoyed to see each other. It turned out that Polly had wanted to leave the hunters ever since her parents had left Simone behind. She knew exactly what had been done and that Simone had never been killed while hunting as they had said. Polly didn't want to stick around, but she didn't have the means to leave either. She took the news of her impending fate rather well and said having her sister was worth turning into a night human. Even better was that once Simone woke from her sleep, she was completely healed and they knew what kind of night human she was. Polly and Simone had left the day before to go meet their father.

"Is that it?" Jen asked from the doorway.

"Yeah," Jax replied as he picked up the box and walked downstairs. Beck's car was waiting in the driveway. Jax dumped his last box into the trunk, which miraculously didn't smell like rotten night human, and went back into the house.

Wes was in the kitchen drinking a bag of blood when Jax came in. He pulled a second bag from the fridge and tossed it to Jax. Jax just shrugged and opened it. It turned out that after his night human side was activated, blood wasn't as bad as it was before. Not that he had drunk fresh blood yet, but the bagged stuff would do. He had so many fears and reservations about changing, but it didn't seem that it was going to be anything like he expected.

"So you're still leaving with Jen?" Wes asked after he finished the bag in his hand.

Since the visit with the fey, Wes could no longer enter Jax's mind. Jax had a feeling it upset his father, but he didn't let on. Jax had told him verbally that he was leaving, but he had a feeling the old vamp was hoping it wasn't true.

"I can't stay here. I need to have my own place," Jax stated. And that was true.

His father used Simone to turn Jax into a monster, and to save her life Jax would do it again, but he couldn't stay there with him and the vampyre. He didn't trust them. Any of them. Surprisingly, turning into a night human hadn't changed that part of him. In fact, it changed very little beyond the physical. He didn't crave blood, though it did taste better now, and he didn't grow power hungry either. He was still himself.

"Beck made sure Jen's place was within the borders of our territory," Wes replied.

Jax knew this much, too. He was taking control of his life, but there were still other laws to attend to, like not going in other clans' territories. Jax was a vampyre no matter how he didn't feel different. There were rules he'd have to follow to stay alive.

"Clan meetings are Sunday night, and you'll be expected to be there," Wes told him. "There are several blood banks near your new place. If you'd rather stop back here, I keep the fridge always stocked. Don't let your thirst get out of control."

Jax nodded as he turned to leave. They had already been over all that before, but he knew Wes was just trying to protect him. Even if Jax couldn't trust the vampyre, he was still his father.

"If you need me, just call," Jax said as he made his way out of his father's home.

Jen smiled at him as he hopped in the car. "I don't know how you got Beck to loan you his car for the week."

Jax grinned. That one was easy. Jax had traded his motorcycle with Beck's car on the promise he would stay in town and out of trouble while Beck visited his mate. For some reason Jax wasn't just free of his father's commands and eavesdropping, he was also now free to see through magic, like the kind that kept Mei hidden from his thoughts before. As soon as Jax remembered, he knew he now had the best bargaining chip to use with Beck to get his way.

"Oh, I forgot to tell you one other part with the fey," Jax said as he drove down the driveway of his father's place and out onto the road into town. "When Polly turns into a night human, my hunter side that is keeping her human will be released."

"Okay, that makes very little sense." The wind was blowing her hair all over the place, but she was watching Jax in confusion. Jax smiled. She looked so much like Jade. He was happy she finally got to meet her when they had picked up Polly.

"Just go with me on this," Jax said. "The deal I made only temporarily used me to anchor Simone's powers.

When Polly joins her clan and turns into a night human, her hunter side will seek out Simone's to become one. That will leave mine to do the same. I know Jade doesn't want to be a night human, so I asked the fey to send my hunter side to you. They said it has to be my sister, which I assumed meant blood. They said it would work. You'll be a hunter with the hunter curse to keep your night human side away for as long as you live. You won't ever have to worry about your night human side breaking free."

Jen's eyes bugged out of her head in shock before she started squealing with joy. She took off her seatbelt and threw herself across her seat to tackle Jax with a hug. He swerved a little bit, but his night human senses tended to leak through into his day human form, and she wasn't going to cause an accident.

Jax smiled at Jen as she sat back in her seat, still grinning from ear to ear. Everything was going good for both of them. He was starting a new life in an apartment with Jen in the city. His plan to keep Jade safe and give Jen the life she wanted at the same time had worked out perfectly, and he even saved Simone in the process. He hadn't thought this was how everything was going to end up, but it did. Life was beginning to look up. Yep, he was definitely brother of the year.

ACKNOWLEDGEMENTS

To you, the reader. <u>Thank You</u> for taking the time to read this story. If you liked it, please leave a review on your favorite online bookseller (or all of them!) and connect with me social media. The greatest help you can do to keep a writer going is to support them by spreading the word about their books.

Also I would like to thank my editors and cover designers. Thank you so much, Kathie at Kat's Eye Editing, Melissa at There for You Editing, and Ashton Brammer. They work so hard to get you guys the best book. A thank-you to my *AMAZING* cover artist Jessica for such a pretty cover- doesn't she do great work!! I'm beyond fortunate to have found these wonderful professionals to work with.

I'd also like to thank my hubby – who is the only reason I actually even published. He does all the behind-the-scenes effort to make this work. This would be so much harder without his help. So thank you, B. for pushing me off the deep end (or the cliff as I see it sometimes). And a great big thanks to my little munchkins who keep me going from before the sun comes up 'til long after it sets. Love you AK, KB, and EM.

<u>Thank you so much for taking the time to read my novel!!</u>

ABOUT B. KRISTIN MCMICHAEL

Originally from Wisconsin, B. Kristin currently resides in Ohio with her husband, three small children, and two cats. A former cell biologist, she now does the mom thing of chasing kids, baking cookies, homeschooling her children, and playing outside while writing full time. She is a fan of all YA/NA fantasy and science fiction. Find her at www.bkristinmcmichael.com and Twitter, Facebook, Instagram, and Goodreads under
B. Kristin McMichae

www.ingramcontent.com/pod-product-compliance
Lightning Source LLC
Chambersburg PA
CBHW061135200626
46817CB00016B/1643